Throwback

Jack Remick

Throwback

And

Other Stories

Jack Remick

Quartet
Seattle

Jack Remick

Throwback
and
Other Stories

Lemon Custard

In August, on the farm, after wheat harvest it was always hot. And windy. On hot mornings, you saw the heat roll up like huge waves on the highway, deep water mirages in the blister of the wind and the hot pouring of air through open windows.

My Grandpa was a big man who chewed Days Work tobacco. He kept a quart coffee can under the front seat of his green Chevrolet to spit in. And he was a silent man.

Even with three of us in the car when he drove us to Liberal, he made me and Nancy sit in the back seat. Be quiet. Be still. But he was not a mean man. He believed in order. You don't run two sections of wheat farm without order. Grandpa drove us to Liberal because, he said, the wheat's in and you two have been good even without your mama here to keep you in line, so we'll have some ice cream.

I knew it wouldn't be just any old kind of ice cream. It would be lemon custard ice cream. It was fast, that drive from Plains to Liberal.

It was a fast highway and even on the fast highway there were the jackrabbits who tried to out run a Chevrolet gunning along at 75 miles per hour and they always failed and when they failed, the radio, set to the news, always the news because you don't run two sections of Kansas wheat without market news and weather news and commodity news—pork bellies and the price of wheat per bushel, the radio shot out a blast of static, zap, like one of the ray guns in the comic books Nancy and I read, and you heard the thunk of a dead jackrabbit and if you dared to sit up and look out the window, you'd see the gray and white fur ripped and streaked with blood.

And then, as the Chevrolet rolled on West, the red disappeared and all you saw was the bump of fur on the blacktop and then that too was gone.

Are you two doing all right? Grandpa asked. He watched us in the mirror, Nancy in her white pinafore and black Mary Janes that Mama bought before she left, and her hair pulled smooth with Snow White and the Seven Dwarves barrettes, and me in my overalls just like Grandpa wore down to the tiny watch pocket without a watch. I knew that one day I'd have a gold pocket watch on a gold chain just like Grandpa had.

Yes, Grandpa, Nancy said. We're all right.

Because she was two years older than I was, she did the talking when we were together.

Butch, you need a shot from the jug?

No, Grandpa, Nancy said, he's all right.

Grandpa never drove anywhere in his Chevrolet or in either of the pickups without a gallon jug wrapped in burlap and dipped in the horse tank after he had filled the jug with ice cold well water and while he drove— either in the trucks or the combines or the tractor pulling a plow, he had a way of holding the jug in the crook of his left arm and drinking from it. When he drank, he always left a taste of tobacco on the rim of the jug.

You sure? He asked. We still got half an hour to Liberal.

We're fine, Grandpa, Nancy said.

2

She bounced her new Mary Janes, the toes raking the back of the seat.

In Liberal, it was hot and the streets full of mirages that shattered when semis flooded out of them and women in their Sunday dresses walked in the sun wearing floppy hats with bouquets of flowers in them.

At the ice cream shop, Grandpa parked and shut down the Chevrolet and turned and said,

Well, let's look at you. Nancy, straighten your belt sweetheart and Butch, tie your laces.

He can't, Grandpa, Nancy said.

He can't tie his shoes?

No, Grandpa, she said. He's too little to tie his own laces.

Well, we'll see, Grandpa said.

He opened the door and turned me in the seat and he squatted in the sun and propped my right foot on his knee and he tied my Buster Browns with the brown laces and then he looked at me and smiled and there was a little brown streak of tobacco at the corner of his mouth and he said,

You look like a trooper, Butch.

You look like a trooper, Nancy said.

Okay you two, Grandpa said, enough. He took my hand and waited for Nancy to slide out of the back seat and then he closed the door.

The three of us with Grandpa in the middle, walked into the ice cream parlor that smelled of milk and baked sugar cones and chocolate sauce. A man behind the glass counter said, Howdy do. He wore a white apron and a white hat and his hair was very black.

Grandpa said, Let's have three double Lemon Custards.

My favorite, the man said.

He flipped open the freezer top and dipped the scoop into hot water and loaded fresh baked waffle cones the color of brown leaves with double scoops of Lemon Custard and handed them one by one to Grandpa who handed one to Nancy and then one to me and the last one he took for himself.

Careful, Butch, Grandpa said.

He won't spill this time, Nancy said.

That's my man.

Grandpa drew from a coin purse he kept in his right front pocket.

That was a magical pocket and it was a magical coin purse, because it held an endless treasure of the half dollars that Grandpa gave us when we were good or when we went home after harvest. He paid the man and we sat in the ice cream parlor chairs of bent white wood that looked like the desks they made us sit in Sunday school. I licked at the top scoop and it was sweet and smooth and lemony enough to make me want to eat it all at once, but we only got Lemon Custard a couple of times each summer and last time I ate it too fast and Nancy told me I had to make it last and so now I licked at it until the custard dripped down on my fingers and onto my overalls and the top of the cone went soft and Grandpa wiped my mouth with a napkin and he said,

How you doing, Captain?

He's doing all right this time, Nancy said. He won't gobble it like a little pig this time.

Not what I'm worried about Nance. I'm afraid it's gonna get away from him before he gets it all down. I guess it takes a long time to learn how to eat a Lemon Custard double scoop, doesn't it, Captain?

Eat faster, Butch, Nancy said.

No, I said. I'm not gonna.

I'll tell Mama, she said.

She won't do anything, I said.

Butch, don't argue with your sister now.

He won't argue, Grandpa, Nancy said.

She licked her Lemon Custard for a while and then she said,

Grandpa, when is Mama coming back?

Umm, Grandpa said. Well, I don't know, Nance.

Why did she go away?

Well, baby, sometimes people have to go do that to get square with themselves.

What does that mean, Grandpa? Get square?

Butch, you're losing that cone. I guess a double is just too much for a little guy.

And he wiped at my mouth and the custard ran down and slatted on my Overalls and Nancy laughed.

Botch's a piglet, she said.

Don't call your brother names.

He is a little piggy pig. Look at him. Look at me. I don't spill.

Nancy was as fresh and clean as when Grandma put that dress on her and there wasn't a drop of yellow custard anywhere on her hands and her hair was still neat and her mouth wiped clean.

Well then, I guess we're done here, Grandpa said. Just then my cone caved in because I grabbed it too tight and it cracked and the Lemon Custard spurted out but Grandpa saved me with another napkin.

Yeah, it's definite, he said. Next time either you grow a foot taller or you get a single.

You ought to give the little piggy his custard in a dish, Nancy said. He's too little for cones.

You too little, Butch?

He's too little, Nancy said. And she got off her ice cream parlor chair like a big girl and dropped her napkin in the trash.

For a couple of honyonks, you two are pretty good, Grandpa said.

What's a honyonk, Grandpa?

I'll tell you later, Grandpa said. We better head on back to Plains. I see some weather coming.

The Pig

I remember the squeal of the pig when my Dad slit its throat and then hooked the pig's shank with steel spikes and raised the pig up until the gusher of blood poured into the blue porcelain basin.

Then, as if the last drop of blood carried its last muscle twitch, the pig stopped jerking and hung there by the hooks in the tendons of its hind legs like a black and white balloon.

My dad, hands bloody wet, stood very quiet holding the blade that sparked bright from the haft down to three inches of blood covered steel and then he wiped the blade on a white towel and sheathed the knife and he handed me the towel and said,

Wipe your face, Butch, you're got his blood on you.

The towel. Soft and white and clean except for the smear of blood. I touched the towel to my face. Small spots stained the white and my dad said,

You got it, son.

He spread the pig's legs with a metal bar that locked into the spikes digging into the hocks and with a long slender knife, he laid the pig's belly open from the slit in its throat down to the sack drawn up tight where you saw the twin pearls of its testicles in pink.

He's a big one, Butch, Dad said. A good one. He laughed. You're too young still for this, way too young.

No, I'm okay, I said. I held the white towel and smelled the warm blood rising from the catch basin. In the blue porcelain the blood turned purple.

Drag that basin out of there, Dad said. You're white as a cotton ball. Yeah, your Mom is right, you're not ready for this stuff. Go on back up.

I'm okay, I said. Where do I take it?

Take what? He asked.

The blood.

Just slide that basin out from under the head 'cause I'm going to gut him and I need room.

Squatting, I slid the blue basin out and across the wooden floor, a screech of metal on wood, of metal on the nails in the wood that raised the hair on my neck and Dad said,

Jesus Christ. And he laughed.

As I tugged on the basin, blood sloshed, alive and very red, very dark, and it slopped up and out and onto my hands and Dad said,

Your mama needs it all for the blood sausage and what you leave on the floor's no good to man or beast.

Yes, Papa, I said. Feeling the vomit boil up in my throat, I gagged, because the blood coated my hands, sticky blood that felt like drying paint and I wanted it off. I wanted it all off and so I grabbed the towel with the streaks of blood from the knife and the splashes of blood from my face and I wiped at my hands and at the fingernails where the nail joins the cuticle, wiped at the little rivers of blood that had burrowed into my skin and just then Dad slit the belly and the pig's insides flopped out and hung in a pink steaming mass just above the floor until Dad shoved his body against the guts and lifted and with his left hand slit the last flesh holding the pig

8

together and in his arms, with his knife, there was a bulging bundle of animal insides that looked nothing like the pig, nothing at all and just then, Mom came down to the shed.

I've come for the blood, Gerald, she said.

She was smiling, her teeth white, her hair, black as coal, pulled back from her face. In her hands she carried a gallon milk jug. She wore a blue dress and a white apron and black shoes and she looked like an angel and she said,

How are you doing my little man?

I wanted to cry. I wanted to hand the bloody towel to my Dad. I wanted to crawl into her arms or hide under her apron and feel her hands stroking my head.

Butch's a little tender, Verda, Dad said.

I told you.

Well, he has to learn. It was a good lesson, weren't it, laddie?

Laddie, Mom said. A little Scottish laddie at his first butchering. The blood, Gerald? I'm ready to cook.

She poured the blood from the basin into the gallon jug she had brought from the house and then she carried it away and Dad squatted and looked at me and said,

You can go on back if you need to, son.

No.

It's all right. Next year, when I butcher, you'll be a year older. Blood is a hard thing for a man to deal with. But you have to get used to it. Maybe not this year.

No, I said. I want to stay.

Sure?

I'm sure.

He smiled then and stood and said,

9

Then I need you to stand up beside me and pull your weight.

The knives. The saw. The sound of metal teeth chewing through the chine.

The pig split in half, each half hanging with ribs and backbone and the small litter of sawn bone on meat and then on the butcher table Dad cut the large chunks of the pig into loin and ham and ribs and shoulder and head—its snout black and white—and feet clipped of their hooves lay like four slivers of white bone beside the liver, still a hot and red clump, and the heart and lungs and spleen—each part named when Dad cut it out and rolled it in butcher paper and labeled each package and then the pig was gone.

And on the butcher table only small packages of brown paper each with a name on it: Chops. Spare ribs. Shoulder roast. Liver. Heart. Loin. Loin. Loin. Dad said,

We freeze it all but the hams and bacon. Those we take to Roy for smoking.

He wiped his hands on his overalls where streaks of blood covered the small clingy remains of the pig and he tugged a cigarette from the pack of Lucky Strikes he carried in his breast pocket and struck a match to the white cigarette in his lips and he exhaled and the smoke smelled sweet and good and then he squatted on his haunches and I squatted beside him and as he smoked he said,

This is a filthy habit, Butch. I don't want you to smoke. Do you hear me?

Yes, sir.

I ought never to have started. Your mama wants me to quit but some things are harder to quit than others and this is one of them.

You don't drink anymore, I said. You quit.

Just barely, he said. Your mama made that clear as daylight, didn't she?

Is it okay for me to drink when I'm old enough?

Dad took a drag of his Lucky Strike. He exhaled. He looked at me and there was a softness in his face.

He said, Well, a snifter never hurt a man if he can control his desire, son. But if he loves the taste of scotch whiskey, he'll never stop wanting it. Me? I'm one of those who loves it. God damn, do I love it.

First Blood

My first blood was a harvest day in August on my Grandpa's farm. All the men—my grandpa, my dad, my uncles, the hired hands who came up out of Texas and Oklahoma for the harvest—were out on the combines cutting wheat. Grandma's job was to take care of us all. Every day she fixed dinner. Dinner in Kansas means the noontime meal. Supper is the evening meal. She fixed dinner by first slaughtering six pullets.

It was hot, I remember, dry and windy the way weather comes down in Kansas in August and across the prairie you saw the wheat bow down to the wind that sifts through the grasses then spring back up.

Killing. First Grandma caught up the pullets in a catch-pen made of wire, herded them to death in a circle, cutting them out of the flock like a cowboy cuts a heifer from a herd and when they were trapped, she reached into the pen and snatched up a pullet and wrung its neck with one quick flick of her wrist and the head snapped off.

Grandma, chicken in hand, flicked the open-mouthed head at her bitch, a huge-fanged German Shepherd named Lucy. Lucy sniffed at the bloody, soft feathered neck, then gulped it down in one mouthful and looked at Grandma who said, Good Lucy.

Lucy wagged her long fluffed tail that beat like the pendulum of a big clock as she waited, eyes bright and expectant, for the other heads.

Grandma flung the pullet out onto the hard-baked chicken yard where the other fowl strutted pecking at corn and wheat heedless of the silent headless bird flopping its life out in a gusher of blood.

She snatched the second pullet from the pen, snapped its head off and the head fell into a heap of dust and blood.

Grandma was on the fourth pullet when, out of the corner by the silo, just where the fields of wheat stubble started, the pickup, a black Ford with a special bed, screamed into the yard and the driver's door opened and Harold, my uncle, my mother's first brother, his face grim and suntanned said,

Mom, call Doc Witham.

There was no Why? There was no What?

Grandma left the pullets, she left me, and she zipped into the house while Harold unlatched the tailgate of the pickup.

I watched as he crawled in beside one of the hired hands who lay in the bed. I saw blood and raw meat and torn Levis.

Harold said, Jackie, you go with your Grandma.

But I hung back, breathing faster than I'd ever breathed as the man groaned.

Harold cut the pant leg off. Pieces of bone stuck from the man's leg and the foot was skewed and blood seeped out of bite marks as if a huge monster had mauled him and then, finding him not tasty, spat him out almost intact. Except for that leg.

Jesus, he said. Trying to sit up, he groaned again and cried, Oh Sweet Jesus, it's gone.

No, it's all right, Harold said. You'll be all right. Doc's on his way.

The man flopped back onto the bed of the pickup and lay silent, his arm flung over his eyes, his mouth moving.

Jackie, run in, tell Grandma to tell Doc to say put. We're comin' in.

But Grandma was already on her way calling out that Doc said to bring him in and Harold slammed the tailgate shut just as Grandpa skidded up in his Green Chevy and burst out of it and said,

Hoddy, how's the boy?

Hoddy was Harold's nickname. No one but Grandpa and my mother called him that. Harold shook his head.

Shock, I guess, Harold said.

Christ, Grandpa said.

He jumped into the pickup and I climbed in beside him and Harold stayed in the bed and nested the wounded man's head on his lap as Grandpa gunned the engine and hit the unpaved road that led from the house to the county access road and then down to the highway that headed into Plains.

Is he going to die, Grandpa? I asked.

He looked at me.

Jackie, what are you doin' here? You're not supposed to be here.

I want to come, I said.

Damn, he said.

I looked out the rear window, saw the blood and the bone of the man's leg and the thin skin of his face that Harold shielded from the sun with his own straw hat.

Will he die, Grandpa? I asked again.

14

He might, Jackie, he's in a bad way.

What happened to him?

You don't need to know that, Jackie.

Tell me, tell me, I said.

He got his pant leg caught in the combine's chain gear, Grandpa said. He got careless and it caught him and it chewed him up and you oughtn't to be here, so you keep quiet and keep out of sight.

I huddled down against the door of the pickup and listened to the high hard whine of the engine and the whir of the tires on the pavement and the howl of wind boiling through the cab until Grandpa wheeled the pickup into the slot behind the Plains Hospital. He wasn't out of the truck a second before the hospital door popped open and a man pushing a gurney sprang out and Harold helped him pack the wounded man onto the white sheeted gurney and then they all disappeared into the hospital.

Son of a bitch, Grandpa said. Son of a bitch.

We sat side by side, Grandpa and me, in the waiting room on blue-backed chairs with chrome legs and hard seats.

Harold paced outside the hospital door smoking, his head bowed, pacing and pacing until Grandpa got up and went to him and laid his hand on his shoulder. Harold dropped his cigarette—Camels, he smoked Camels—and came back inside and sat, open-legged on a chair, head between his knees until I had to pee and Grandpa took me to the restroom at the end of a long hot corridor because he had to go too and it was something standing side by side with him peeing and he looked at me but he didn't smile.

When we came back, Harold sat, eyes closed, his head pushed against the wall.

Are you all right, son? Grandpa asked him.

My fault, Dad, Harold said. I just know.

You can't take the blame for something another man does.

He's eighteen, Dad. Hell, he doesn't know anything yet.

Still, Grandpa said. Still.

We sat for three hours before Doc Witham showed up wearing a white gown smeared with blood.

He was a short man with a bald head and a pencil-thin black mustache that looked like it had been painted on his very dark skin.

Paul, he said.

Doc.

It's not good, Paul.

How bad?

Boy's lost a lot of muscle off that leg.

Did you, uh....?

No, Doc said. I packed him in ice, sending him to Liberal. They might be able to do something over there.

You think so?

Well. Doc shrugged and looked at me. Hi, Jackie, he said, then to Grandpa. Both bones are shattered.

Both bones?

The tibia took the worst of it. The fibula's .... well... We'll see. They might have to put in a steel plate.

Oh, Grandpa said.

Damn, Harold said.

Harold, Doc said. You doin' okay? All right?

I'm doin', Harold told him.

In the pickup, out back of the hospital, I sat between Grandpa and Harold. They were quiet, and then Grandpa started the pickup.

Grandpa, I asked, What's going to happen to him?

I don't know, Jackie. But you know what? We missed Grandma's fried chicken. Are you hungry?

You bet I'm hungry, I said.

Maybe we ought to stop at the drugstore for a grilled cheese and a root beer, Grandpa said.

Prom Date

The night Darlene Davis told me she wouldn't go to the Prom with me we were in her Mother's Chevy in a vineyard off Bethel Avenue. Darlene sat facing me, her knees up on the seat. She wore jeans, white tennis shoes, a red sweater. A white blouse under the sweater was open at the neck. She had a half-drugged look in her eyes, a kind of look at me too hard and I shatter look. I glanced away, because even at 17 you know when your heart is being broken.

The car was hot. The radio down low. KFRE. Black blues just coming into the white bread world of our Valley. A bridge over the river that flows and takes its time to get to the sea.

I never learned to dance, Darlene said.

I don't care, I said, I still want you to go with me to the prom.

She looked away. I felt her eyes lift off my skin the way you feel the scab break loose from a slow healing cut. Okie girls have this thing they do with their eyes. They can cut you deep or turn your blood so hot your skin blisters. Then, she let those blue eyes dart back at me.

You don't really mean it, she said.

I mean it.

I better get home, she said, the milk's gonna clabber.

Darlene, I said. I lunged for her hand, stabbing at the car keys in the ignition before she hit it. Her hand was hot, moist. The Valley spring night cool. The car heater on low.

Darlene Davis was an Okie girl who said 'ain't'. I was an Okie boy who said 'ain't' but who played the piano, wrote poetry, ran with both the elite of Sanger High and with Linard Pope whose name was a synonym for wild. Darlene was an Okie girl with twin younger sisters at home and she come out to buy milk for them and then she stopped by to tell me she couldn't go to the prom with me.

She waited. Defeated. Her head rested on the steering wheel. I pulled her hand off the keys.

I want you to go with me, I said. I've already rented the tuxedo.

Those people are different, she said. She looked up through the windshield at the world we lived in— vineyards, sky, dirt. A few stars. Not much. I saw the sparkle of tear in the corner of her eye and then she sniffled.

You think I care what they are? I asked her.

I still can't go with you, she said.

Why not?

Because.

Then I did something stupid, something I regret. I spend a lot of my life regretting my smart mouth that sometimes acts like it's connected to my brain by knee-jerk stupid wires. Is it the dress? Can't you afford a prom dress?

She tensed up and then she was sobbing and I put my arm around her shoulders and she leaned into me. She felt so real and solid and I felt very tender right then.

We had kissed twice. The first time by accident almost—one night she brought me home, I don't remember why but as I got out of the car, I touched her and when she didn't jump away, I kissed her. Nothing came of it.

The second time, there was more to it. More of that hunger for each other, the kind of hunger you have when you're 17 and you can't wait for the feel of the skin and the hot, wet smoothness of a ready mouth. That time, she melded into me like she belonged there and we made out for a long time not knowing what would happen or where it was supposed to go next. That night, in the vineyard, I didn't touch her body. I wanted to, but her mouth was enough because there was something delicate and fragilel about her—something that wasn't there in the Okie girls Linard lined up in the vineyard the way butchers line up cattle to slaughter them.

So I asked her to go to the prom with me.

It was always chancy—to ask cold—but she said yes. Maybe she wanted to make love as much as I did. Maybe she was curious and 17 and the moment was right and she wanted something but something held us back that night. Maybe because she was an Okie girl. Maybe because I didn't know what to do with her. I didn't know what her experience was. What? Less than mine? More than mine? I guess then was when I knew that I felt something for her I'd never felt before.

So there, in the mom's Chevy, in the vineyard, in early Spring, I held her shoulders and tried to be convincing.

No, it's not the dress, she said.

What is it then? I asked her.

I've gotta get home with the twins' milk. It'll spoil.

She pulled away from me. I insisted. There was something about Darlene Davis that made me want to be with her. Maybe it was our accent—the way we both said cain't. Maybe it was something deeper.

Maybe it was knowing that our parents grew up smelling dust and tasting dirt blowing and learning how to work in the orchards and vineyards for a few pennies a day.

I remembered the song, Hey Okie, if you see Arkie, tell'im Tex's got a job for'im out in Californy, pickin' up prunes…

I'll buy you more milk, I said.

My mom will kill me, she said.

Darlene, it's kinda late to back out.

She froze then. She slumped again.

I'm afraid, she whispered.

It's a dance.

You'll be ashamed of me.

What?

Ashamed, she said. She looked at me, hard, the eyes wet, the mouth trembled.

How can you say that?

You know.

Look, I said, if you want, we don't have to double with John Townsend and Michelle. We can go alone. Just you and me.

And then what?

What do you think?

I know what they'll think.

Tell me.

They'll think you asked me because I'm easy.

Her words slammed into me. My chest tightened.

Easy? You think I asked you to go with me because I think you're easy?

I hear talk, she said. I listen. Janice Beck told me…

21

Janice has a big mouth.

She said you're all over a girl.

Jesus Christ. Janice wants you to be all over her. She's like that. She screws every guy she goes out with and then claims she's a virgin.

Did you screw her? She said that up at Pine Flat, Ditch Day, you ripped her bra and panties.

Darlene, look... None of that matters. You and me...

It matters to me. It matters to me what people think. I'm not a pushover.

I never said you were. Look. You don't want to go to the prom because people will think I screwed you. Are you a virgin?

I've gotta get the milk home, she said.

If you are when you go out with me, you'll be when I take you home.

She hooked her thumbs on the steering wheel at an awkward angle, her palms turned to the wind-shield.

Okay, she said.

You'll go.

Yes.

I touched her hair. It was stiff with spray, but the back of her neck as hot and wet. I rubbed her skin. It was good sweet skin. She looked at me. I saw the ache in her mouth, her eyes, her lips were wet. She wanted me to kiss her.

Instead, I touched her lips with my finger tips. She closed her eyes.

I'd never mess with your reputation, I said.

People like us don't get two chances.

Okay, I said, take me home.

That's my line, she said.

She parked on Richard Street two houses down. I got out. She rolled down the window. The night was chilly, but I felt the heat rush from inside the car, heat scented with her perfume.

I'll pick you up at 7:30, I said.

She nodded. The Chevy—a new, loaded 1958 Impala—throbbed around the corner. Then Darlene was gone.

I still smelled her hair spray. I could almost feel the silk of her skin on my fingers. Darlene Davis was my date. She was an Okie virgin who was afraid of my reputation as the bad boy who ran with Linard Pope and who also ran with some of the establishment kids. I was a mixed breed and I should be going to the prom with someone like Julie Wilson whose father was a manager for the phone company.

As I entered the house, I heard my mother playing the organ. How Great Thou Art. My mother spent her time either on her knees praying or playing the Hammond. It was an obsession with her. A way to atone for all the sin in the world. The more she played, the closer she got to god because god created the Hammond to make up for creating Lucifer and Okie boys who ruin the daughters of the church.

Darlene wasn't at school the next day. It was 3:30 PM when I got home. My mother was playing the organ. There was a lot of sin in the world and if she was going to make it right, she had to let the righteous hymns boil out of her like etching acid to strip away the lust and gluttony and other transgressions that batched up like too-thick pancake batter on a cold griddle.

I went to my room and huddled on the bed. And then the music stopped.

My mother was at the door to my room. This was a strange thing because she never stopped playing when I was in my bedroom. She said,

Darlene Davis called.

What'd she say?

She can't go to the prom.

I didn't say 'shit'. I wanted to say 'shit', but when I said 'shit', my mother always went to the organ and played I Come To the Garden Alone. So I swallowed and picked up the phone and called Darlene.

Her mother answered.

This is Jack.

Hi, she said. Her Okie accent gives it a 'hih' like she's saying 'hat' without the 't' on it.

Can I talk to Darlene?

She's not here.

Where is she?

Went up to San Jose, she said. Her granny's took sick.

When will she be back?

I can't say.

She hung up. My mother was back at the Hammond playing The Old Rugged Cross.

In my room, I pulled the tuxedo off the rack in my closet and tried it on. It fit okay. I looked good. I'd have looked a lot better with Darlene on my arm.

She was the first woman who ran out on me. Okie women have a way of doing that. They grab your heart, twist it up into knots, say they love you, then go off with some cowboy to do the things they never would do with you. My heart has a lot of knots in it.

Wet Wednesday

Roosevelt Way is wet today. Puddles of rain collect like oases in a black desert. The water glistens from corner street lamps still on because of the dark, overcast, rainy Seattle sky, but angled light shoots into the eye with stingray crispness.

I leave the cats, Ginger and Eliza, sitting in the window watching me trudge through the rain. It has fallen for two days. I feel the wetness in my shoes as I walk to Café News for my morning cup of espresso and a copy of the New York Times. Double shot this morning, I tell John Faure, the owner. He works the morning shift alone from six till nine. He always wears a blue sweat shirt with a Seattle Seahawks logo. Jeans and white sneakers. He always wears white sneakers. His hair is curly, black. Stacy, John's girlfriend, sits at the coffee bar by the telephone reading the morning P-I. The paper rustles like a dry leaf in the wet steamy air of the café. John twists the espresso machine knobs. A hiss of steam shoots into a cup. He grins at me. Slides the coffee across the bar. I stand beside Stacy while I wait.

She has black shoulder length hair. She wears a soft black cashmere sweater and black tights. She has on a pair of soft shoes, the kind of shoes modern women wear when they want a little comfort with their fashion. A generation ago her mother would have told her to wear sensible shoes. Pumps, maybe, flats. She folds the PI to the Wednesday fashion section. There is a full page ad for the Bon Marché. I did this display, Stacy says, pointing at the ad.

Stacy is an artist. She sculpts, paints, draws. She could be the Picasso of her generation. But like all artists in the 21st Century, she has a money job doing something she doesn't like. She creates fashion displays.

A quick check of the ad shows two women posed in winter wool suits. Behind them there is a roll-top desk. A mirror hangs over the desk so you see their outfits from the front and back. On the desk there is a flower vase with a white rose in it. The vase takes a flash of light on its round belly, shoots it back at the camera so the eye focuses at the center of the ad.

Very cubist, I say. Stacy grins.

You like it?

It's good. Pablo would love you.

Don't be cynical.

I'm not being cynical. You painted a Picasso with a camera. That's good.

John leans on the bar. For a moment the café is quiet. No one in. No one out.

How's the novel coming? John asks.

It's getting there.

Awright. Bagel?

What's fresh this morning?

Currant and cinnamon. Cream cheese. Special for a buck seventy-five.

Deal, I say. The bagel. And a copy of the New York Times.

I dump in a packet of sugar. Sip the coffee. It tastes tart the way I like it. Strong. Right on the edge of burned. Is the vase silver? I ask Stacy.

26

What? She looks up from her paper.

The vase, in the display. I just wondered if it is silver.

I think it is pewter.

You told me it was pewter, John says.

Yeah, she says. It was. She goes back to the paper. John looks over her shoulder toward the street.

I sip John's coffee. Taste the sweetened bitterness. Stacy crinkles a page of the PI. John leaves to go slice a bagel. You hear the knife click through the bread on the plastic cutting board. The fridge kicks in with a knock, then it smoothes out to a long bleating chug chug chug.

Leaving Stacy to her paper, I take my coffee to a window table. A string of cars congas its way down Roosevelt in a spray of mist. The tires grind the rain into a veil. The shush of the tires on concrete is the steady hiss of rain snakes crawling out of the morning commute. Then the door opens. A woman in a blue rain coat stomps in. Rain spatters the floor. Drops of rain shatter the fluorescent light on her coat to a dusting of diamonds. John smiles at her. He is always smiling, always a little bit speedy, a little bit high. Stacy glances up. She rattles a section of the P-I. I take another sip of coffee. It's sweeter now.

The woman in the blue coat orders a double tall latté. Decaf. Non-fat. I laugh. Why bother? Sugar. Coffee. Fat. Chocolate. My four basic food groups. She's too thin anyway.

John rings her up.

Wet, she says.

Um huh, I hear John say. The woman glances in my direction. She smiles that early morning smile that doesn't say much, but it ferrets a nod out of me. The nod says, 'you look good.' The smile replies, 'Are you a nice man?' I want to be nice. But I don't think I am. Not really. Not since I bogged down in the middle of my novel.

She sips foam off the latté. Caps the cup with a plastic lid. As she heads for the door, I notice that her slip, an inch of lavender silk, hangs below the hem of the blue coat. I catch Stacy's eye, drag her to the slip. She arches an eyebrow. Smiles. See. Not nice. If I finish my novel, I might be nice again. But for now, I notice every flaw. In everybody.

The woman exits to a gray BMW parked on Roosevelt Way. Lights on. Wipers swishing. Engine running. A stream of gray exhausts into the rain. The café door squeezes closed. A gust of cold wet air sweeps into the room. I shudder.

The café warms up again. The coffee is strong. I remember that I'm supposed to be a writer, but instead of hammering at the keyboard, instead of working on my dialogue I'm looking at Stacy and John huddled nose to nose across the bar muttering in low voices. I would like to be that young, to feel new love surge through me once again. He cants his head as if to ask her, 'do you mean it?' They are too young to know the empty feel of a king-size bed at three A. M.

The last half inch of acid coffee etches my tongue. The heat slips away.

Stacy laughs. John touches her hand. He raises it to his lips. She strokes his face. He holds her hand like it's a small bird. I hope he's a gentle lover who takes her to the edge then eases her down. I think he is. Some mornings I see it in the blush in her skin. Too much love. Not enough sleep.

Hey John. He looks up. Surprised that I'm still there. I'll take the bagel with me.

What?

Yeah. I'll just take it home.

The bagel. He's forgotten all about it. But he wraps it in plastic, drops it in a bag, hands it to me. Stacy's face is flushed. She smiles at me, a distant empty smile that doesn't see me or hear me or notice anything about me. I'll see you tomorrow, I say. Stacy drops back into the P-I. I don't remember ever seeing that look in any of my lovers' eyes. That Stacy look, just now, before she went back to the P-I. I don't remember ever seeing that flushed skin. I don't remember that kind of smile. Maybe I'm not good enough to make a woman smile like that.

Outside, the rain is still falling. I trace the path I've worn in the concrete from my house to Café News. Every morning I fight my way home to the computer, to the novel.

All the way back, I see Stacy and John—young love— in black and blue. And then at the corner of Twelfth Avenue and Eighty-ninth Street, I remember the New York Times. Damn.

It's a Rubicon now. Do I go back for the Times? Do I need proof that the world is going to hell? It will take me an hour to read the paper. It will take me a year to finish the novel. It's always the same questions—do I cross the street? Do I open the door? Do I click on the machine? Write the big sex scene? Or do I spend the rest of the day in the crushing ignorance of a man without a New York City newspaper? And what about the cats? Did I feed them? I'm sure I fed them. Early. Or did I?

I make a decision—if it stops raining in thirty seconds, I go back for the Times.

Still holding the cinnamon-currant bagel in its paper bag, I stand on the sidewalk in the rain counting— twenty-nine, twenty-eight, twenty-seven...

Priscilla Reads Wet Wednesday

We agree to meet at 1:00 PM. Priscilla says she'll read my story, Wet Wednesday. To pay her back for reading the story, I'll drive her downtown to the Joshua Green Building where she works on a history project. It is 1:07 when I stop in front of her house. Heavy rain. Huge splattering gobs drum the roof and windshield of the Subaru and tattoo the umbrella Priscilla shakes before getting in the Subaru.

Hi, she says.

I hand her the yellow folder. I put all my work in yellow folders now. I used to color code by draft—sketches in tan manila. First rewrite in blue. Second rewrite in green. Third run through in Red folders, and Reading draft in Hot Pink—ready for the presses. But with the computer, what's a draft? A draft used to be a retyping of the whole thing from first page to last. A lot of it never changed, but you retyped it anyway just to feel it come alive again. The computer changes the way we think about art. About writing. About ourselves.

I wrote Wet Wednesday sitting in the Café News coffee house before it burned down. This just after my first workshop with Natalie Goldberg in Taos. I came home ready to write a memoir because she inspired me to think about the things close at hand such as my life, my wife, the women in my life, my writing.

I wrote <u>Wet Wednesday</u> in the time it took to drink a double tall non-fat latté, wrote it out longhand on my yellow legal pad, and then typed it up and put it in the computer, as they say, and worked it there for a long time.

So what's a draft?

Machines change art.

I rewrite everything on the machine except when, for some obscure reason having to do with my platonic view of truth, I rewrite, from scratch, re-invent, re-create again longhand on the yellow pad in writing practice at Louisa's Bakery Café on Tuesdays and Fridays. But there's the loss—the evisceration of the art, the feeling that truth is abandoning me at the table, leaving me empty, alone, very unpeaceful.

Priscilla reads aloud as I drive. At first it's annoying because the wipers make noise, the car makes noise, the rain makes noise. Her voice is a low muttering. She's a poet. She needs to hear the words, feel them in her mouth. I want to tell her to read louder so I can hear it, but I don't. I drive. She's doing me a favor. I drive.

We take Aurora over the George Washington Memorial Bridge on the Lincoln Highway known to everyone in Seattle as the Aurora Bridge. We forget why and how things get names. Like Captain George Vancouver who renames Tahoma, calls it Mount Rainier for no good reason. We call things what we want to. Like Alice in Wonderland the words mean what we want them to mean.

Just across the Bridge, just as we pass Canlis Restaurant where, in the evenings, limos and chauffeured Mercedes Benzes park in waiting, Priscilla lets out a whoop.

She's laughing.

She reads more. Muttering to herself all the time.

The laughter gets louder. God this is funny, she gasps.

We turn off Aurora onto Wall Street by Seattle Center. She laughs. Reads a few lines, laughs louder. Tears in her eyes.

That's just the way it is, she says. Exactly the way it is with a writer.

I turn left on Fifth Avenue. Pull into a parking spot at the corner of Fifth and Bell while Priscilla finishes the story.

When she gets to the last paragraph she pounds the dash. The last paragraph is where the narrator remembers that he's left the New York Times at the Café. He says, *Do I go back for the Times? Do I need proof that the world is going to hell? It will take me an hour to read the paper. It will take me a year to finish the novel. It's always the same questions—do I cross the street? Do I open the door? Do I click on the machine? Write the big sex scene? Or do I spend the rest of the day in the crushing ignorance of a man without a New York City newspaper?*

So you like it? I ask her.

She sniffles. Wipes at her eyes.

It's terrific, she says.

Now Priscilla has just three levels of critical evaluation.

<u>Good</u> which means you better take it back to the computer and rewrite it a couple dozen times.

<u>Excellent</u> which means it's readable but there's still so much work to do you'd be ashamed to send it out the way it is.

And, last, she's got—T<u>errific.</u>

Terrific is an A+ followed by her admonition: Don't change a word of it.

When Priscilla first read <u>Falcon and Kress</u>, a novel of mine, I got a <u>Good</u>. I knew I was in trouble so I rewrote it half a dozen times before I got an <u>Excellent</u> and then rewrote the rewrite four or five more times before that <u>Excellent</u> turned into a <u>Terrific</u>.

The <u>Terrific</u> meant <u>Wet Wednesday</u> had passed beyond words into emotion, and the best and purest kind of emotion—Laughter.

It's the highest accolade for a writer, laughter . You don't buy laughter, so I am honored that the writing god has let me have that little piece of joy—just a peek at the great beyond, that place where the door opens and out roars a belly laugh.

Okay, I say, do I send it out?

I love this story, she says.

She closes the yellow folder, rests it on her knees. Pats the folder the way a naked lover pats the smooth behind of the loved one after sex, and she smiles.

Yes, she says. Don't change a word of it.

I start the car. Wend my way down Fifth Avenue to Union Street, make a right, pull into a half-hour zone. Priscilla gets out, opens her umbrella.

Thanks again for driving me, she says.

Thank you, I say.

I drive home. A long, slow drive.

It has taken me two years and three months to finish <u>Wet Wednesday</u>. It was never longer than five pages. The finished story is now four and one-third pages, 1486 words. I owe it to Natalie Goldberg who, in Taos, told us to write about everyday things. That was the last workshop she taught that was pure writing. It was in

December, just before Christmas. After that she got tired or she burned out—writers and teachers burn out like booster rockets on an orbital shot. After a long, fast, hot burn, they quit working. She started mixing in a lot of non-writing, non-essential stuff borrowed from her life as a Buddhist monk. *Write about the thing in front of you,* Natalie told us. *Keep the hand moving, show the detail, because God hides in the detail. Nabokov said there is just an S between* cosmic *and* comic. So <u>Wet Wednesday</u> is a pure story triggered by the last pure writing workshop Natalie Goldberg ever gave.

It is a good story about a lonely man in a lonely place watching young lovers moon across a coffee bar while it rains outside.

I park the Subaru in its usual place in front of my house and switch off. Switch off the wipers, switch off the radio, switch off the engine.

I sit in a warm, quiet place listening to the still heavy rain hit the metal roof of the Subaru, and then I pull the keys.

I grab my pack and the yellow folder with the laughing copy of <u>Wet Wednesday</u> in it.

I go into the house and email the story to Lois Petersen in Canada. She has a little magazine called <u>Words</u>. That's just right. Words. I'm a writer. I write words. Lois answers an hour or two later. Her email tells me it'll be one to four weeks before I hear her decision.

That's all right. I don't hold my breath anymore. I'm past that. I heat water for a cup of tea, pull up PCH, a novel I'm working on that Priscilla tagged as Excellent, and I type at the sixteenth rewrite of Jonny's first sight of Pacific Coast Highway. It's a turning point in his life. He's the protagonist of the novel. An Okie boy from Turlock,

California. He watches the waves off Malibu. He doesn't know that in a year, he'll meet Bea and his life will go all to hell.

Throwback

I remember the first time I saw her. A woman who floated on a sea of her own perfume. Free. Vibrant red hair like the mane of a Teutonic warrior priestess. Atavistic and primitive as if this were the one Tacitus wrote about—the mother of the collapse of the Roman Empire. She might have been a Hun, one of the wild women who ran screaming and naked into battle.

You can't tie a woman like that down. Words fall off her like rain on oil cloth. You say, 'God, you look good,' and she turns her back. You say, 'You smell nice,' and she laughs at you. How do you pin down a woman whose ancestors put the fear of god into Julius Caesar?

A white straw hat, a sundress the color of calendulas in bloom, a bicycle riding down a chestnut tree lined boulevard in the heat of summer. Quiet and hot and humid.

I was stunned when she wheeled up in Sproul Plaza and slid off the bike like a lizard sliding off a hot rock. Glints of sweat shining on patches of sun-drenched skin. She smiled at me. The dismissive smile a woman masters after a certain age.

I held the door open.

Thank you, she said. A voice as rich in timbre as her hair was deep with the hues of bloody sunsets. She shoved her sunglasses up into her hair.

Sproul Hall was icy that day. Everything in the elevator was chilly all the way to the seventh floor. She watched the floor marker, her eyes flickering, a lizard's quick green eyes, and when the door opened I held it for her. Followed her. Caesar would have done it. I had to do it.

Natalie Cassidy, the department secretary, sat at her desk working a crossword puzzle from a thick book of puzzles and chewing the end of a Number 2 lead pencil raw. A worried look on her face, her mouth tainted with red dots of eraser.

Shit, she muttered and then, looked up. Oh god, I'm sorry, I didn't see you.

The woman in the yellow sundress held her white straw hat in front of her.

I'm Ellen Kole, she said. Sunglasses up on her head, green eyes taking Natalie in like bait.

Professor Kole. Natalie stumbled around her desk bowing like a novice to the Pope. Forgive me. I didn't expect you till tomorrow.

Of course, she said.

Professor Ellen Kole smiled. Her voice sent warm gushes rushing up my spine and electricity over my skin. It had been a long time since I heard a voice that flowed electric over my skin.

Natalie was still quaking. Professor Kole turned to me.

We won't say a word about your foul mouth, will we?

No ma'am, I said.

Since you seem to belong here, she said, we might as well meet formally.

She held out a hand, a smooth sun-darkened hand cast in gold with glimmers of stones, diamonds, sapphires, booty from the sack of Rome, a thousand years of plunder on that skin.

I'm Edward, I said. Edward Hall.

Oh god, Natalie collapsed on her desk. Both of you on the same day.

Edward Hall, Ellen Kole said. The Edward Hall?

Um, one of many, I said.

I'm sorry, Natalie said. This is too much.

What is too much, love? Ellen Kole said. She glanced at me, green eyes roaming all over me—knives carving a deer carcass. I shivered, felt naked and alone and vulnerable. A Roman with a Hunnish blade in his heart.

Well, I mean two prize winners on the same day, right here, Natalie said. Jeez. I'm sorry.

Ellen Kole laughed. Just show me my office, she said, and in the morning we'll start all over.

We faced one another. Her office set on the opposite side of the hall from mine. From the doorway, I watched her roll her chair out, slide into it with the grace of a leopard on the prowl. She was ready for action.

The distance between us wider than a canyon and formal. Very formal. A few feet, but years apart. She had her proclivities, I had mine.

I work from ten at night until six in the morning.

She lived in her office, slept on a futon that she rolled up in a corner during the day.

I ate at Chez Antoine on the Round, she packed box lunches and bought a small refrigerator that rattled when it came on.

She was a maniac who wrote so fast the nib of her pen tore the paper.

I work like the builders of the pyramids—one word at a time until I can stand back, God's plan in hand, to see my ivine creation.

She threw away her autograph pages with the trash every day after she typed them up.

I save every scrap of paper, every idea, every note and keep it all in neat folders in a disciplined filing cabinet. Color Coded.

But still, the more I saw her, the more I wanted her, even when the fall brought sweaters (angora) and heavy skirts (peasant style) and dark evenings. Her skin still glowed health and screaming Gothic warrior maidens.

A woman like that exudes desire, and freedom, and the inevitable—fear. She infects a man with his own desire until he understands why Caesar had to subdue the demons of the Marches.

Everything changed on October 15th, the day she broke her leg riding her bike into a chuck hole on Campus Parkway. From hole to chestnut tree to pavement, a bloody crash.

I'm so clumsy. I visited her as she lay in bed, at Community, her face scratched, her lower lip bruised, her mane flaming like fire on the cool white pillow, her aura palpable. Wounded and irresistible.

It's a compound fracture.

The city's to blame, I said. They'll have to buy a new bike.

I suppose, she said. Thank you.

For what?

For coming. No one else from the department has come.

They'll be here, I said.

How did you know? She asked.

You didn't open your door, I said.

Oh. Thank you, Edward.

She shook my hand and gave me a name. Her hand trembled. In her hand I felt fear. I touched vulnerability. She was alone. Desperate. All that energy and fire and she was alone.

You'll be in here a few more days, I said. I'll take your classes.

You don't know what I teach, she said.

Prize winners are interchangeable. They won't even know you're gone.

You do have a bit of hubris, don't you, Edward?

Yes I do, I said, but when you're good you can take a few liberties.

Talent forgives being an asshole, she said.

Something like that.

***

For three days, I brought her flowers and chocolates. She cried. No one had ever brought her chocolates, and no man had ever given her flowers. The fracture didn't want to heal. Ellen hated the cast, hated being locked down.

Your students...

I know, she said, they've all come to see me.

All six of them, I said. And they can tell the difference between you and me.

It's not a popular seminar, she said. But they told me you are wonderful.

Watch out, Ellen, I said, I might replace you permanently.

You could never replace me, Edward, she said.

***

The cast stayed on for eight weeks. After that she walked with a cane. The cane disrupted everything. She couldn't ride a bike and she had no car. I rented a Volvo station wagon. She rented an apartment. I hauled her from hospital, to apartment, to department.

I'll never walk straight again, she said. Something about my bones not healing right.

You'll be fine, I told her. It's taking a little longer than usual, but you'll be fine.

I hate optimists, Edward, she said.

***

On January 6th, All King's Day, she didn't answer her door when I came for her. I called. No answer. I called her office. The phone rang, but no answer. At the department, I asked Natalie if she'd seen Professor Kole.   Not today, she said.

Do you have a key to her office?

Natalie, still awestruck by achievement, had never been able to talk to me without blushing. She fetched a key from a box, handed it to me, and returned to her puzzles.

Ellen's office was dark. Cold. Blinds drawn.

She lay on her futon. Naked. Blood on the floor. Blood smeared over her body. Streaks of blood painted her forehead, her chest, her belly. She had opened her veins. Not in the usual way with a slice across the wrist but with a pearl handled straight razor she had cut the left arm from armpit to elbow lengthwise and she had opened the femoral artery on her left leg, the broken leg, the leg that did not want to heal, and then she had wiped the razor on a paper towel, closed it and laid it on the floor beside the futon. The paper towel lay crumpled in her blood.

The small refrigerator clicked on, rattled like a beast in the hollow darkness of the office.

I squatted, soles of my shoes in her blood, and I felt her skin. Cold.

I turned on the light, looked for a note, a letter, a tape, but there was nothing.

Her peasant skirt lay on her desk and on the skirt her white underwear, bra and panties, and, stacked beside her skirt, a thick manuscript. The pages were bound between purple covers and had been punched with three holes and bradded with brass studs.

Across the cover page, in bold yellow print, she had written, The History of My Suicide, by Ellen Kole, Ph.D.

The Taurus

He was quiet. Too quiet for a man his size. He sat in the sun on a wrought iron chair at a wrought iron table staring at the coffee cup in front of him.

On the street, traffic worked the twelve o'clock rush like slow syrup dribbling out of a plastic bottle. The hiss of tires, the sometimes whack of a door closing, the occasional sharp shock of a backfire like a firecracker. The sun, perched overhead, was hot, even for August. August. Not a good time of year. Hot and humid. The kind of weather that drives you crazy.

I sipped at my iced tea. Took a refill when the waiter came to drop the check for a grilled cheese with ham.

How long's he been there? I asked.

Who?

The big guy at the corner table, I said.

Oh yeah. I don't know. A couple of hours. Today.

Today?

He's here every day. Sometimes from eight-thirty to five.

All day?

Yeah. You need anything else? I've gotta settle.

I paid the check, left him a tip that was big enough to keep him from whining at me.

At home, Laura was waiting with scotch on ice. She looked good. Fresh. Like she'd just exercised and showered. Bright.

She's tall enough to play basketball, and muscled enough to take the fight out of life. We'd been married six years, but things were fraying at the edges. I didn't do anything right. She was impatient. The weather didn't help.

What's on your mind? She asked me over grilled chicken and pilaf with a salad dressed in pine nut, oil and vinegar. The salad was better dressed than I was.

Nothing, I said.

You're acting weirder than usual.

Later, in bed, I thought about the big man on the corner. It was too hot to sleep, so I fidgeted, felt Laura's heat beside me. In August we both slept naked so her skin stuck to mine making it hard to shift around without ripping something.

What's going on? she asked me.

I told her about the big man and the waiter. How he sat at the table staring at the cup, not looking at anything but the coffee.

What were you doing in Belltown? she asked me.

I had a lunch date with a client.

I thought you had lunch with Bob on Thursdays.

He's in New Mexico, I said.

Oh. I forgot.

Are you all right?

Why?

I don't know. Maybe it's just the weather.

I looked at the Taurus this morning, she said.

Oh?

I think I'll buy it. It's used...

If you want it. It's all right.
It's too hot. I think I'll sleep in the basement.
Do you want company?

On my way downtown, at eight o'clock on the Route
73 bus, I was already thinking about the big man, so I
checked in at work, took calls, read messages, and was in
the café at nine o'clock. I sat down to a croissant (currant)
and coffee (filtered). When I'm out, I always drink
American coffee because I get pissed off paying three-fifty
for half an ounce when I can get eight for a buck and a
quarter.

He ambled in at nine-ten.

He was a huge man with huge ears and a huge nose.
Big beefy lips made his face look like the work of a mad
sculptor on speed. His shoulders were big enough to take
an ox yoke. Thick neck. Like a football lineman. Huge but
graceful. Like a dancer. Big men who make waves will do
that—pace their way along because if they jerk around
fast, they step on the little ones, the slow ones, the
children. Huge but graceful.

He eased himself into his wrought iron chair at the
wrought iron table. The waiter brought a foamy cup of
coffee. He paid the three-fifty. He drank it a sip at a time
then he just stared at the cup from nine-twenty-five on.

By eleven I had read three newspapers, drunk four
glasses of iced tea and was going nuts.

There were two ways to go at this. One was to walk
up to him and ask him just what gave him the right to
bug the hell out of people. Two, which seemed more
sensible, was to let him bug the hell out of me.

Because he was huge and because I didn't want to get
stepped on, I said nothing. I paid the check, left a smaller

than usual tip guaranteed to tick the waiter off, and went back to work.

That evening, Laura was all over me like a duck on a June bug. She wanted to know where I'd been. She'd called work four times. She wanted to know what I'd been doing. Who was I with.

What are you asking me?

Your weirdness, she said.

Meaning what?

Meaning I don't know you anymore. That's what.

You slept in the basement last night, I said.

It was hot.

You think there's something going on?

You never listen, she said.

Did you buy the Taurus?

Yes.

Well?

It's okay. I like it.

~~~

Laura slept in the basement again. I didn't sleep. I get that way. Obsessed. He was there, in bed with me, heavy enough to weigh me down, his massive ears like peacock fans, his heavy lips like a hog's mouth, his shoulders pushing into my pillow.

I was gone before Laura came up. I knew that she'd taken sleeping tablets (prescribed by her psychiatrist) and when she did that she was groggy all morning. I didn't go down to kiss her goodbye.

At nine-thirty, he sauntered into the café. He wore the same suit, the same tie, the same shoes. But his eyes were puffy and his skin flushed like he'd been crying. His coffee. The stare.

I called the waiter over.

47

He looked at me the way a man looks at three day old road kill he's just found stuck to his radiator.

Does he have a name? I asked.

Some people respect it that a man has to earn a living, the waiter said.

What?

He wiped at my table with a clean white towel. Some people know what's right, he said. You come in here, you take up space, and then you disrespect me and everything I stand for with a pissant little tip.

I'm sorry, I said. I was short yesterday.

You don't owe me, he said. I just have to pay rent and make car payments, and buy food once a week. So you don't owe me, you owe my landlord and the bank.

Look, I'll make it up.

Some people just use places like this the way bums use park benches.

What about him? I asked.

The waiter sniffled at me. Looked at the big man. Him? Well... He shrugged. He doesn't stiff people just to be mean.

The big man stared at his cup. Hands folded in front of him. And then he stood. I checked my watch. It was ten-thirty. He reached into his suit jacket for bills. Without counting, he dropped money on the wrought iron table and then he walked into the street into a BMW convertible running in the curb lane on Fifth Avenue. The BMW slammed into him and drove him back up into the café tables and blood slung out like water from a broken hose and the BMW spun around, brakes, tires, metal howling and flipped up on the sidewalk slamming wrought iron tables into the windshield and the leg of a wrought iron chair tore loose and flew spear-like into the driver piercing his throat and nailing him to the leather seat.

Jesus Christ, the waiter shouted. He grabbed at me, hands like claws. Oh god. White. Lips trembling. Oh Jesus. Frozen.

I pulled him loose and ran to the big man who sprawled across an upended table on his face, the back of his head bleeding, cracked open blood red and I saw that the hair on his neck was long and silky. A stream of blood pumped down the back of the suit jacket and then his right hand twitched, scratching like a crab on the concrete, before going still.

I heard the driver of the BMW. A guttural wail. An animal call. Help. I ran over to him. He was wild eyed and bleeding, pinned down, lips moving like a fish in water and then his eyes closed and his mouth sagged open.

The quiet, before the sirens came, hung like crystal suspended over a marble floor. Then it splintered in a shrill cachophonic rain.

~~~

I was late getting home. The cops like to hang onto witnesses. I talked to three policemen and a detective and I was very tired. I called Laura to see if she wanted to come into town, but got the answering machine. Three times, I called. I had missed my bus so I hired a taxi which cost me more than I wanted to pay.

The house was still when I opened the door. No smells. No lights. No music. Nothing. The kitchen door was open. I looked in the back yard, then went inside, called down to the basement for her.

She wasn't there.

In the bedroom, I stripped, slipped on the Super-man silk robe Laura bought me for my birthday, then went to the bathroom.

She lay in a bathtub full of water the color of blood, her face half gone. The wall to her right had shattered when the bullet powered through her head and smashed into the tile.

The Taurus, a nine-millimeter, the weapon she had bought for protection, lay on the floor beside her left hand. She had taken off her wedding ring and placed it in the sink and her Chinese red silk robe lay folded on the toilet seat.

Anton—A story triptych
Anton Remembered

Before leaving for the night, Anton blanked the screen on his desktop computer. He then clicked his leather briefcase closed. The snap was the last sound in the office and Anton was the last one out.

The elevator, crowded but quiet, slipped down from the twenty-first floor of the Rainier Building. Perfume, the scent of fading cologne. Anton cleared his throat and watched the floor marker tick down, fifteen, fourteen...

On Third Avenue, Anton joined Mary Ellen, who worked at the Financial Center, and who met him every evening for the walk through the deep ache of winter that poured from the cold of the snow and ice. The trees, with their vestigial summer leaves, cracked in the gray-black afternoon wind of traffic.

Mary Ellen, tall, chunky, Adidas and smoke gray nylons, matched Anton, stride for stride.

Walking under the gray sky, Anton glanced up startled, as if seeing the sky for the first time, a sky, seamless and gray, that slid over the world brooding with its great wings in the dark winter where the muted thunder of Sea-Tac bound airplanes crumbled onto the rooftops, down onto the street echoing like the roar of snarling beasts. The thunder seemed to crack the white crisp of frost on the curb then roll into the swallowing darkness like a tongue disappearing into a cavernous mouth.

At Third and Union, just before dipping down to the tunnel, where the buses ran for rush hour, Anton looked up. On the Sound, boats skimmed the skin of the abyss carrying their cargos to the fires and the ice and the prisons of time where bones break and bend, then grow soft before slipping into the dust of spring.

Clattering, quiet clattering, the escalator carried Anton and Mary Ellen into the artful shadows of the underground.

What a terrible day. Anton shrugged. Mary Ellen shook her head. The black scarf around her neck fluttered like a dying bird.

Yes, Mary Ellen replied. Layoffs...

That's not what I meant.

Oh. Mary Ellen turned her head away.

They offered me a promotion. I don't know.

Anton set his briefcase on the sidewalk. He dropped thirty-five cents into the coin slot of the vending machine. Lifting the door, Anton picked up the second paper in the stack. The Times.

How's Susan? Mary Ellen asked.

She's fine. Anton folded the paper in thirds, then placed it under his arm.

Here's the Express. Mary Ellen touched Anton's arm Anton picked up his briefcase and followed her aboard.

* * *

It was late when he turned out the desk light. Late, and Susan had been asleep for hours. Listening to her soft breathing, Anton undressed in the dark. He nestled against her back. He felt her heat. He smelled her nighttime scents, the fresh showered scents of shampoo and powder. His hand snaked around her waist, hesitant, then pulled back when she muttered a deep sleeping ummmm.

* * *

Anton awoke before the alarm went off. The needles of sleep still pinned his eyes, and the pain of waking was on his tongue and the crease of the pillow on his cheek.

The dark aroma of Starbuck's sifted through the light to settle over him. A cloud of awakening smoothed the taste of toothpaste and the coffee steamed over the Post-Intelligencer full of its darkness. Anton folded the paper to the comics but could not laugh.

Good morning, Susan said. Anton looked up, startled by the faint hiss of her feet in gray and white rabbit fur running over the tile floor. Through a blue velour robe the whiteness of her thigh shot out like a shaft of morning light. Anton felt the thickness in his groin, the sudden stab of swelling flesh.

He opened the newspaper to an inside page, to a photo, to a drawing.

They got another one, he said, I guess, a prostitute on Aurora. Butchered her. Like a hog.

She bent over, the velour robe falling open to reveal the swell of her breasts and over the swell the delicate pink lace of a nightgown peeked. She rested her hands on the paper to read about the woman found in a Queen Anne park, headless, naked, arms severed. Susan shuddered.

Oh, why does this keep happening?

Shrugging into his gray topcoat, then pulling on his gloves, Anton said, There is just so much hate.

Remember the Beatles? She closed the newspaper. The love you take is equal to the love you make?

See you this evening. Anton opened the door. The cold frost on the lawn spoke white hellos to him as he crossed, his feet deep, taking the white on the soles of his shoes to the corner then down the street to the bus stop on Fifteenth Avenue where Mary Ellen, cigarette sweet in the late dawn light grinned and said,

Good morning, Anton.

Anton smiled. Lovely, he said.

And then, Anton remembered. Oh! He gasped.

What? Mary Ellen's hand clasped his arm.

I left the work I brought home last night.

You'll miss the bus. If you go back.

I'll call Susan. Maybe she'll bring it down.

They fell into the silence of friendship, the silence of habit and ritual, the silence of knowing the scent and touch of one another. They waited for the bus, waited to ride the fifteen minutes through the gray and snow white frosted air, through the smell of cars leaving their entrails in the morning.

Anton

Anton closed the door of his gray Chevrolet. The door clicked shut with a muffled thunk. Anton then opened the door to the house. He walked into the underbelly of the white elephant he had paid too much for.

But Anton, a pale man with thinning hair, was neither happy nor sad. This evening he was perplexed and neutral. His wife, Susan, was away visiting her mother. A mother in law of middle nuisance value who came to visit only at Christmas.

Susan liked to visit her mother. The visiting perplexed Anton only because he didn't like to sleep alone. The fact that Susan was mute in bed and made love only twice a month had little to do with Anton's perplexedness.

In general, Anton was content. Neither happy nor sad. Just content.

He hung his gray overcoat on the mahogany and brass rack in the foyer and sighed.

Then he turned on the tv and as it ran something he didn't pay any attention to, he opened the freezer, taking out a turkey and brown gravy dinner that he microwaved on high for eight minutes.

Anton put the empty tv tray in the garbage and was about to loosen his tie when the back door bell rang. Anton went to answer it.

Through the milk glass of the back door, Anton saw the silhouette of the woman. Turned profile, her nose jutted out from her face, echoing the slight downward slope of her breasts.

Her hair was up on top of her head in a French twist, so that the total effect was of a cameo of a fin-de-siècle woman.

Anton opened the door.

Chris, he said. His voice thin and high.

Chris, hand outstretched, held a plate, and on the plate there was a small slice of pie. Behind Chris, the porch light gleamed, casting her face in the shadow, the ridge over her eyes turned her face dark and empty, but she twisted into the light and smiled.

Anton, I know Susan...

Visiting her mother...

Chris stuck the pie toward him, jabbing it like a sword, at Anton who backed away, as if the pie were a snake.

Here, Chris said. She shoved past him into the kitchen where she set the plate on the glass topped table.

Not too much of a mess, Chris said. Are you eating?

Am I eating?

Susan said you always eat tv dinners when she's away.

I stopped at the Oxbow for a steak.

Good. She was worried about you when she called.

Susan called?

Yes. At three.

Oh. Anton sat down. He bent his neck to one side then to the other.

Stiff? Chris said.

Long day, Anton replied.

You need a hot bath and a good night's sleep. I have to go. Chuck is waiting.

Chris, Anton said.

Yes?

When you talk to Susan tomorrow, tell her I'm all right.

Chris laughed.

Alone, Anton pulled his tie off. He rolled it up into a loop like a brown cinnamon roll then he set it in the middle of the table beside the apple pie. He smelled the cinnamon that seeped out through the sugar on the crust. He leaned forward. The scent of clove and the tart odor of apples filled his nostrils.

Anton shoved the pie away. Then he went to the bathroom. He stepped out of his brown pants and he peeled off his shirt.

He faced the mirror. Running his fingers through the hair on his chest, thick wiry hair, ape-like in its thickness. He forgot about his body, from time to time. Forgot that he had it, that it had hair and bones and sweat glands and urges and desires and wants and needs.

He forgot about it, it was like it didn't exist most of the time.

The shower ran hot, the water boiling up in clouds until the air was thick with lung filling steam. Anton stepped out of his underwear, boxer shorts, white with a red trim around the waistband. The hot stream of water hit him, burning. The sudden scalding made him wince, but he stood firm, letting the water run over him until he grew used to it, until he turned red, and then he increased the hot until it stung.

In a few seconds, Anton was bright red. The black hair on his chest looked like thick black worms working their way through a white mass of dead skin and then Anton rinsed away the soap and he stepped out of the shower, holding a soft brown terry cloth towel to his hot face.

Dropping the towel, he reached out to the mirror, but stopped his hand when he saw the shape with no edges, the fuzzy shape blending into the gray of the steam and the crystal of the mirror.

Anton wiped away the moisture on the mirror.

He turned down the bed. The crisp sheets opened like white orchids. Hand on the chest of drawers, Anton hesitated. Deciding not to put on pajamas, he slid into bed. The reading lamp cast a pale yellow circle on his pillow, on his head. He turned the lamp on high. Without Susan next to him, there was no reason to leave it low. But there was nothing to read and he was about to turn off the lamp when he realized that he had left the tv on.

Tossing the covers off, Anton got out of bed. The trip an added weight that made the rest of the day seem like a huge stone. The tv, just too much, how had he been so stupid to leave it on.

He stepped out of the living room and into the sudden glare of the light from the kitchen and the refrigerator door was open and Anton said, Susan?

The door closed.

Chris, Anton said.

Chris looked at him. Her eyes narrowed, her right hand up to her mouth. Anton remembered then that he was naked.

But he was also open and vulnerable and alone and what was Chris doing in the kitchen.

I...I told Susan... She asked me to check to see if you had milk for your cereal.

You talked to her again? Anton said.

She just called. She said you might be asleep, would I check for milk and you have milk.

I bought milk today, Anton said.

Oh.

But I'm glad you check.

I have to go, Chris said.

Anton hesitated. Chris, at the kitchen door, turned to him and waved a tight, tentative goodbye. Anton felt a sharp fire in his groin.

She shut the door. He turned off the tv. Then he went back to the bedroom and lay down but his head was full of naked Chris, Chris who would tell Susan how Anton had surprised her in the kitchen, and Anton lay wide awake until after two in the morning, still seeing Chris naked, still seeing Chris look at him.

In the morning, Anton poured milk over his cereal. He opened the newspaper to the business section and then set the comics aside for Susan before he remembered that she was gone.

He was half way through his grapenuts when the kitchen door opened.

Chris, Anton said. He stood. He wiped a dribble of milk from his chin. Chris, I'm...

I'm sorry, Anton, Chris whispered. Her lips moved as she spoke but her words were a rasp. She rushed to the table. She sat down. I'm so sorry if I embarrassed you last night. She put her face into her hands and her hands into her lap. She wore a blue velour robe that gaped at the throat as she leaned down.

Anton put out a hand. He drew it back.

I'm the one, he said. Embarrassed. Oh god.

Chris lifted her face, her eyes behind the splayed fingers, then the fingers fell away. There were tears in her eyes.

Chris? What is it?

I'm so lonely, Anton, she said. She leaned into him, her arms at her sides. So lonely. It's so lonely out here. No one, no one except at night and then it's too late.

Too late?

Chris pulled free. She wiped at the tears with the sleeve of the robe.

It's always too late, she said. I have to go.

Chris... Anton reached for her, and she was up against him. He held her, his arms around her, feeling her warmth, the soft, yielding flow of her body against him. She smelled fresh, fresh like perfumed soap and oil.

You're so warm, he said. But you're trembling.

Oh my god, Chris said. She pulled away. Her hand on the door knob, her legs parted the blue velour and Anton saw the flash of her thigh. And the scent of her body rose up to him, and he wanted to touch her, to peel away the blue, to touch her white.

He checked his watch.

He saw the hand on the 4. He was late. He was never late. He was going to be late.

Chris, he said. His voice was thick and full of phlegm.

Her mouth crushed his, her teeth cracked into his and he felt a sharp pain that he swallowed as he drew her close until the fell the robe open and her naked skin rubbed against him. Her hands unbuttoned his shirt, peeled it open to reveal the black hair on his chest, and he drew her against him, crushed her breasts as he held her close to kiss her mouth, this time with his lips and his tongue and his whole body.

***

Anton, she whispered.

He hung up the phone.

What did he say? Chris asked.

Nothing. I told him I would be in at noon.

What are we going to do?

Nothing.

Nothing? Nothing at all?

No. Chris this has happened. It happened to us. And it will stop. It will go away. Susan...

I don't want it to stop, Anton. I didn't want it to start, but now I don't want it to stop.

I'm sorry, Anton said. He turned his face toward her. She lay on her side, facing him, her breasts covered with the white sheet, her hair spread out around her head on the pillow, her throat flushed and red, her pale mouth pink. Anton fixed on her eyes, fixed the eyes in his memory, fixed the memory the way a camera fixes a photograph. For good.

He touched her lips.

You have soft lips, he said. Very soft lips.

***

What is it? Susan said.

Nothing, Anton replied.

You seem different.

I am different.

Susan laid the comics on the table. Anton, she said. You are very different.

I was late to work on Friday, Anton said.

Late?

I overslept.

You overslept?

You have to quit going to visit your mother.

Anton. I have to visit my mother.

Yes.

***

Anton started the mower. He made his Sunday afternoon swath through the lush lawn. As he came back to the sidewalk, Chris parked in her driveway. The Cherokee, black and spiked with sun flares, lurched as she set the brake. Chris waved at Anton. He waved back. She disappeared into the house.

Anton finished the front lawn, and then swung around back, picking up the taller patches between the flagstones between the two houses.

Chris waved at him from the back porch. Anton shut down the mower. He walked to the fence. Chris stood drinking from a tall glass full of ice. She wore white shorts that fit her brown legs very tight, and a loose sweat shirt with the arm holes cut big.

Hi, she said.

Hello Chris. Anton leaned over the fence. You look well.

I am well, Chris said. She smiled. I am very well.

What are you drinking? Anton said.

A coke. A very cold, sweet and delicious coke.

Well, I have to finish the back yard, Anton said.

I'll watch. Chris smiled at him. She sipped at the coke.

Anton started the mower. First he cut the edges, making a border. The cut grass, lighter than the taller grass, made a pale green frame around the whole yard. Then Anton cut a diagonal from corner to corner, and then another until there was an X in the center of the lawn. Wiping his brow, Anton then cut the triangles of grass one at a time until he finished beside the patio with the last push and shut off the mower.

Anton put the mower back in the tool shed that sat under the emerald king maple in the corner next to Chris's house and then he went inside.

The scent of fresh brewed coffee filled the kitchen. Susan sat the table, working a crossword puzzle. She glanced up as Anton opened the refrigerator.

I just made a pot of coffee, Susan said.

I was looking for a coke.

You don't drink coke.

We ought to buy some coke, Anton said.

Coke? Really? Susan said.

I think I want a coke, Anton said.

A coke?

Yes, Anton replied. I'm going to quit drinking coffee.

Anton In The Rain

Anton walked two blocks west then turned one block north. Wind from the south lifted the collar of his wool overcoat and ruffled the hair at the back of his neck.

He counted steps as he walked...six, seven, eight, nine, ten and then stopped in front of the gate.

It was closed.

The gate was never closed. Even on windy evenings in March. The mail box door hung open. The box was jammed with mail that had gotten soaked. The ends of the letters sagged, and the edge of one of Susan's quilting magazines had swelled up like a tumor.

Anton set his briefcase down. The mail had never gotten wet before. Before, always, Susan picked it up just as she got home, took it in, sorted it into three piles— Anton's mail, which consisted of a few magazines and the twice monthly letter from his mother in Tucson. Stack two was Susan's—her quilting machines her magazines, monthly bills, and her smattering of what she called Personal Correspondence, while the third pile of mail was that in-between mail addressed to no one, or stamped with the pre-sorted cheap frank.

'I thought you'd like to see it all before we recycled,' Susan had said.

Anton lifted his briefcase, opened the gate with an awkward dip because of the wad of mail in his left hand, and he tried to enter the house but the door was locked.

This is unusual, he said.

He set the briefcase down for the second time. He struggled with the black leather key case in his pants pocket, and with one hand, slid the front door key from the case, and jabbed the key into the slot and just then a gust of rainy wind slammed the door open into a dark, cold foyer.

Susan? Anton said. He set the mail on the small maple table in the foyer. He wiped his feet on the gray mat, and then slipped off his wet shoes, unbuttoned his overcoat, hung it on the mahogany and brass rack just inside the door and then he picked up the briefcase and fled into a dark kitchen.

Through the kitchen window, he saw the lights of Chris's house blazing and bright. In the window, her hair falling down into her eyes as she stood at the kitchen sink, was Chris herself. Anton unbuttoned his jacket. Took it off and shook it before draping it over the back of one of the matched set of four Dragonwood chairs that had come with the kitchen table.

Anton looked around at his own kitchen. Dark. The lights off, the smell of disinfectant sharp as fresh pine pitch.

Susan! Anton called out.

Upstairs, Anton stumbled on the last step when his right foot bumped into something hard and flat. He switched on the small stairwell light—there was a switch top and bottom of the stairwell for safety—and on the floor before him, an open suitcase, his black Airflyte suitcase with the black and white ribbons he had tied on the handle before his last trip to San Jose.

Empty.

He closed the suitcase and set it aside.

Susan? He called again.

In the bedroom, the bed had been made, the coverlet turned down, but, strangely, the clock radio was blank. Off.

Anton's heart raced as he opened the bathroom door. He expected to find something gruesome. Something awful. Obscene. Too horrible to speak out loud.

But the bathroom lay in its shadows, the hollow white tub like a slab in a coroner's lab, and the towels, monogrammed with A and S, were folded over the towel rack on the wall.

Anton turned back to the bedroom.

Susan? Susan? Susan? He shouted the third time as loud as he had ever shouted inside the house.

And then he saw the square gray envelope leaning against her pillow like a tombstone.

Anton sat down on the bed. In Susan's hand, his name had been etched across the face of the envelope in light blue ink. Hand trembling he held the envelope until it shook and when it was about to fly out of his fingers, he took a deep breath and with his left thumbnail slit the flap, plucked out the note, and flipped it open.

'Anton,' she had written. 'I can't go on like this. Not with everything that's happened. I've gone to my mother's. I won't be back. Good luck. Susan.

P.S. Will you call Gary?'

Gary? Anton wanted to remember who Gary was, but his brain fluttered as his eyes roved back and forth over the note. 'I won't be back.

Why won't you be back? Anton said.

He tucked the note into the gray envelope, closed the flap, and set it on her pillow. Then, standing, he slid off his tie, unbuttoned his shirt, shed it and folded the shirt into a neat package that he laid on the bed before he went to the closet for the steel hanger.

As he unbuckled his belt and unbuttoned his trousers, he noticed that all of Susan's suits and blouses were gone.

In fact, the closet was bare on her side from the empty shoe rack on the floor to the hook on the door where she always hung her sky blue house robe. Empty. Totally and completely and doggedly empty. Nothing remained.

Oh, Anton said.

He staggered back, lost his footing, but recovered then and retrieved the hanger and clipped the trouser onto it and he reached for his jacket. His jacket? Where had he left his jacket?

Then he remembered. He had left it in the kitchen. The kitchen where he never left clothing. He had taken it off as he watched Chris next door labor at the sink.

Well. He'd get the jacket later.

He returned to the bed, stared at the blank clock face. He had to be up at 6:00 A. M. in order to catch the 7:15 A.M. express to downtown and how the clock was off.

He searched for the electric cord that lay coiled behind the night table and he plugged the cord into the wall socket and the clock blinked—12:00, 12:00, 12:00 with a mechanical insistence.

Anton watched it. And then he checked is wrist-watch. It said 7:10.

But the clock said 12:00, 12:00, 12:00.

Huh, Anton said.

He rubbed his palms on his thighs. Bare thighs that shocked him—no pants.

Oh my god, he said. He stood, opened his drawer, pulled out a pair of black sweat pants, stepped into them, and, on a lark tugged out the top drawer of Susan's side of the wall length maple dresser...and...it was empty except for his photograph of Susan standing on a beach in Cozumel. She wore a red sarong, white sandals, and her hair was cloud white in the sun, her skin the color of burnished bronze. She smiled.

Oh dear, Anton said. He slipped on a black sweat shirt then walked to the stairwell where he picked up the empty Aiflyte suitcase that had to be returned to its place in the garage.

But in the still dark kitchen he saw Chris across the way. She walked back and forth like a figure in a television set. Framed by the window.

Anton set the suitcase down and went out the front door and down the sidewalk and up the walk to Chris's door where he rang the bell.

Anton, she said. She stood in the doorway. Crying. Eyes red.

What? he asked.

Susan told me she was leaving, Chris said. I'm sorry.

Oh. Yes. She left me a note.

A note?

Yes. A note. She's not coming back.

Chris sniffled, then wiped at her eyes.

Chuck's left me, she said.

Is that why you're crying?

I guess, she said. I told him I had not been faithful to him and he left.

With Susan?

No, Chris said, Susan has gone to her mother's. She paused. Took a deep breath. Then she said, But she knows about us.

Oh, Anton said. Gary.

Gary?

That's what she meant. Gary.

I don't understand, Anton.

Gary is the lawyer who helped her when she was in the accident with beer truck and the school bus.

Have you eaten, Anton?

No. Anton looked at her. She had no lipstick on. No eye make up. Her face was plain but soft and pink despite the reddened eyes. He glanced at her breasts, lowered his eyes to her bare legs, then down to her feet. No shoes. Bright red toenails. He took in her eyes again. She smiled.

Are you hungry, Anton?

I don't know.

Chris looked at him. Still smiling.

It's an hour past your dinner time. You must be famished.

Chris....

I don't want to eat alone, Anton. I never want to eat alone.

Are you sure you want me to come in?

It's all right, she said. It's going to be all right. And she took his hand.

Hair

I didn't want to go in there. Didn't want to see her. Didn't want to feel the things she made me feel so I sat in the Mustang idling it back, then goosing it, listening for the little knocks, the pings, the sounds of metal worms eating the sleeves of the pistons. I loved the live, wild pulse of the mill. But it needed work. We all need work.

She wanted me to meet her at the Lone Pine Motel on North Shore. The Lone Pine was the last of the old-style motels built before the boom hit Tahoe. It had a ranch verandah, log siding, and a view of the mountains from the deck of each room.

A jetty ran out into the lake where, in summer, boaters boated and swimmers swam in the ice blue, ice cold water.

I shut down the Mustang, shut off the radio. flipped my Marlboro out the window. I still didn't want to go in there, but there comes a time when you have to step over the threshold and do what you came to do. I locked the car, took a deep breath and entered Room 7.

Room 7 smelled. Dank, moldy, the smell that fog and mist and winter and water give a place when it's sealed up for a very long time. I sat on the bed smoking and listening for some sign of her in Room 6—a cough, the knock of a chair against the wall, a toilet flushing. I knew she was there. She said she'd be there. She told me what to do and how to do it—check in to the Lone Pine, take Room 7, knock on her door at 8:30 P.M.

I crushed the life out of a half-smoked Marlboro in the Lone Pine glass ashtray, took a deep breath, went out the door and knocked on Room 6.

She said to come in, it's unlocked.

She sat on the bed in a room lit by a forest of tall, thin white candles. Candles—sandalwood—everywhere—rooted on the night-table and the desk, spilling on top of the TV. Even by candlelight, she was one of those women who take your breath away.

No part of her was perfect, but it all came together the way a jigsaw puzzle melds itself into a picture when you fit the last piece in place. Her legs were long, maybe too long, and her neck was thin, maybe too thin, and her face had angles and planes that took the light of the candles like a prism. Her arms, willowy and thin, by themselves didn't make you salivate, but attached to her China doll hands they were statuesque. Perfect. Delicate. And her hair, a tawny, coppery curled sea framed her thinnish face and made her skin glow like waxed marble.

Well damn, she said, I thought you'd decided not to come.

Here I am.

I heard you drive up.

Debra, I said, I don't know if I can do this.

So much for our agreement.

I didn't think you meant it.

There's no one else I can trust, she said. Do you need something to drink first?

I need something to eat first, I said.

Standing she stretched. It was a long leonine stretch like a hot, quiet cat limbering up for the chase. She wore a black skirt and a red scoop neck blouse and stockings the color of a tarantula's belly and high heels that should have crippled her when she walked but somehow she made it all smooth and oily.

The walk to the Smoke House took five minutes that seemed like five years. I didn't want to get there because once we got there we'd have to come back and when we came back I'd have to do what I came there for.

We ate steak and potatoes and salad. She nibbled, didn't say, much but drank two bottles of a Corbiere from Carcassonne until her cheeks flushed blood-red.

That's an expensive wine, I said.

It's a going away present to myself, she said.

Debbie, I said, what you're asking me....

Shut up, she said. She reached across the table and sealed my lips with a long, thin index finger. I don't want to hear it. You came. I need you.

When I offered to pay for dinner, she shook her head.

I'm spending it all, she said. Every dime.

When a woman won't let you pay for her steak and wine, you know you've got trouble.

I dragged my feet all the way back to Room 6. I watched her the way you look at an exotic animal in a good zoo. The way she walked in her high heels each step was as smooth as a leopard's gait and the roll of her hips rominded me of a cheetah in slow motion—timeless and perfect. No words. No touching. Just a lithe stroll back to Room 6 and its candles and its heat.

I'll just be a minute, she said. Look in the bag on the dresser. She disappeared into the bathroom.

I opened the bag and stared down at a plastic pouch and a syringe along with a stretch of rubber tubing and a phial of water and a butane cigarette lighter with a red case.

I set the syringe on the bedside table with the lamp and shook the pouch open and tasted the white powder in it.

It's heroin, she said. Pure, one hundred percent heroin.

I turned. She stood in the doorway to the bath-room.

She wore a white terrycloth robe and a white turban on her head. She had wiped away all her makeup leaving her face pale and naked. No eyebrows. No eyelashes. Her lips were pink and plain and her eyes stark and glaring. In her hand she held a wig the color of tarnished copper. Her hair. Gone.

That's right, she said. All gone. Every hair on my body is gone.

She tossed the wig on the bed She pulled up a sleeve of the robe and held out her arm. The skin was smooth as ivory. None of the small hairs that take light and turn it into rainbows and then she peeled off her turban and I saw her head was bald. Shiny. Not even a single strand of that coppery mane I had always wanted to run my fingers through.

My god, I said.

No pubic hair either.

Jesus. I didn't know. When you told me on the phone, I didn't believe you.

You thought I was a vain, exaggerating fool.

You want the truth....I thought you were over-board on this.

The truth is that until this happened, I thought I could make it. But I can't live without my hair. When everything else was going bad, I always knew that I looked good, that men wanted to screw me. That they were crazy about me. But without my hair...Losing my pubic hair. I mean, without that I'm not a woman.

It'll grow back, I said. It always does.

Bullshit, she said, it doesn't come back for people with what I've got, she said.

Some men are turned on by hairless women, I said.

Are you turned on by hairless women?

You'll be like a little girl again.

A little girl. My uncle liked little girls, she said. For a long time he took me when my aunt was away. When I pubed, he quit. You see? Having pubic hair made it stop. Now my protection is gone....

I took her hand and sat on the bed.

Sit beside me, I said.

We huddled together for a long time. I felt her warmth, felt her tremble as she cried. Her shoulders were thin, angular, bony but somehow she fitted into me like we were made for it. I thought about how it could have been with her.

And then she said, The one thing I needed and he took it. God is punishing me for my sins and for screwing all those guys while I was still married to Larry and for giving him herpes and who knows what else.

There is no god, I said.

How do you know that? How do you know there is no god?

If there were a god he'd have killed me for wanting to be those guys.

You never acted like you wanted it.

This whole god thing is overrated, I said. Who needs a god with a bullwhip to remind you you're a sinner?

You really wanted me? Every time we talked on the phone I did everything but wrap it up in red ribbons and lay it on your pillow. If you'd wanted to, you'd have done it a long time ago.

Every time I listened to you on the phone I jerked off thinking about you naked on a bed with your legs spread wide open.

Really? You jerked off thinking about me? How sweet.

Debbie. Look, come back with me.

And do what?

We'll go back to the City. You move in with me. We'll go places, do things, drink lots of wine. We'll find doctors.

And what about your wife? No. It's too late.

It's not too late.

Listen to me. I... can't... go... on. Okay?

She kissed me. Warm lips, gentle and cruel and so full of promise it made my head swim and I knew then it was over.

Pulling away, she smiled and opened the pouch and filled a big metal soup spoon with heroin and mixed it with water and cooked it with the cigarette lighter and sucked it all into the syringe and set the syringe on the bed and then she rolled up a sleeve and cinched the rubber tie around her arm until the big vein throbbed and turned blue.

And then she lay back on the pillow.

Okay, Max. It's up to you.

Debbie, are you sure?

My hair, look at me. I won't live without my hair.

No. Won't do it.

Max, you have to. I don't trust myself to do it. If I try it alone, I'll make a mess of it. I want it to be clean.

And painless?

She looked at me and took a deep breath and nodded yes.

Let's get married, I said. Reno has places open twenty-four hours.

Do they have twenty-four hour divorce shops, too? Because you'll need a divorce if you want to marry me. But you can't marry me. You're trying to save me. Don't try to save me, Max. You said you'd do it. I trusted you. When it's done, you take everything I brought—the clothes and the bag and the bathroom stuff and dump them somewhere. I want to be an anonymous corpse found at a Tahoe resort.

I'm taking you back to the City.

I don't want to go back to the City, Max, she said. If you leave me alone, I'll do it myself and if I have to do it myself, I'll make a mess of it. I don't want to make a mess.

In white. Her skin. Naked, shiny. She looked little and alone but she wasn't scared. Her eyes said she was ready. Maybe she was right—if I didn't help her she'd find a way to butcher herself. I knelt and rubbed the darkened vein stretching the skin and she slid the needle into the vein and looked at me as I took a deep breath and leaned down and kissed her hairless face for the last time and with my left hand I eased the plunger down until the barrel of the syringe was empty.

Now fill it and do it again, she said, use it all.

***

About 3:30 A.M. I smoked my last Marlboro and the candles, burned down to stubs, guttered out one by one. The rubber tie lay coiled on the bed like the skin of a molted rattle snake. I left the syringe in her arm and gathered up her things—the black skirt and the red blouse, the stockings and the high heels, the copper wig and the rubber tie and I packed it all in the kit she'd brought. I cleaned up the cigarette butts and wiped out the ashtray. I picked the candles off the night-table and the desk and dropped them in the bag along with the rubber tie. There was nothing left of her then.

In the bathroom, I looked at myself in the mirror. Sometimes you can't see the monster under the skin.

From the doorway to Room 6, I looked back at her on the bed. Her head rested on the pillow—naked like a mannequin in a department store window in a display for bedroom suites. Her arm with the spike looked bluish against the white terrycloth robe and there was a peek-a-boo of her knee and a bit of thigh. She looked like she was sleeping.

I closed the door and took the bag to the Mustang and locked it in the trunk and then went back to Room 7. I don't know why. I had nothing there. Maybe I just didn't want to leave her. Maybe I wanted to stay there until they found her. Maybe I was waiting for her to come back. Maybe I just wanted to wallow in a big pool of guilt and regret. *Somehow she got away. Maybe I said no one too many times. Maybe there are some women you never say no to because when they're gone they're gone for good and you'll never know what might have been.*

***

The Mustang has a hundred and twenty thousand miles on it and it still has that ping, that knock in the engine, but it runs okay. I'll wait until it breaks now, won't try to maintain it, keep it up. Just let it run until it stops.

It's better that way. A lot better. Some things you don't want to fix, some things you just can't.

The Starveling

Caller ID said it was Susan. I waited to answer because it was the fourth time in a week she had called and because every time I talked to her my hands trembled and I got short of breath. I let it ring a half dozen times, then the machine kicked in and while she left her message I drank some of the still-warm coffee I'd just poured from a morning pot that had been bad at 7:00 A.M and still tasted like crud at 9:30.

It's Jon, she said, I can't do anything with him. I think I'm losing him. Call me back. Please. Cell phone. Okay?

I finished the coffee, brushed my teeth, took a shower, got dressed, watered the fuchsias and dead headed the window box dahlias. They were in full bloom and cranking out a dozen blossoms a day.

I watched a squirrel claw half a pound of suet from the bird feeder that hangs under the eave by the dining room window and watched him fall off, flying, and hit the ground so gorged on suet and sun flower seeds that he waddled to a tree, tried to climb it, but had to sit on his haunches, belching, half a dozen times.

She answered on the second ring.

I'm glad you called, she said.

What's up with Jon?

It's good to hear your voice, she said.

Same voice I had yesterday.

Don't be that way.

Okay. What's going on?

He won't eat, she said.

Oh.

I'm going to lose him.

Why won't he eat?

I don't know. He's locked himself in his room and he won't talk to me. I've tried...really tried....but he won't come out.

She cried. I watched the squirrel still hunkered down, a glazed look in his eyes, his belly still distended. He staggered onto the patio where he squatted under a deck chair, then, like the air was leaking out of him, he sprawled, feet splayed, tail strung behind him. And then he fell asleep.

Susan said, I'm sorry. I always cry when I talk to you now.

Do you want me to come down there?

I don't know what you can do here.

What is Michael doing?

What do you think he's doing? What he's always done. Nothing.

Well, he's the dad. He should talk to Jon.

You don't understand, she said. All this time and you don't understand.

Tell me, I said.

Jon won't talk to anyone. It's been days. He comes out when I'm in bed. I hear him, but he won't talk to me.

I watched the squirrel who, I think, was snoring, still with his paws out, belly bloated, eyes closed, his body rising and falling. I wondered if he'd ruptured something on all that suet.

I'll come down there and I'll talk to him.

What will I tell him? she asked.

Tell him I'm the love of your life.

He'll like that, she said.

Tell him what you want, I said. I'll be there in the morning.

You don't have to, she said.

***

I caught the 7:30 Alaska flight to LAX. It was fifteen minutes late. She was waiting at the gate, eyes red, hair tousled., I remembered the first time I'd seen her there. Five years. A long time. A long time to have your hands tremble and to run short of breath. Some things you can't help. You just take them as they come.

You don't look good, I said.

I didn't sleep, she said.

She smelled good, like perfume and expensive soap and she wore designer everything. I was crazy about her but I wasn't crazy about her Designer Label Mind.

She drove. Dark glasses. Quiet. It was warm in LA that morning, but as we wandered down the freeway and wound out to the golf course, a breeze kicked up off the Pacific and with the windows down it was cool, just on the cusp of warm, sort of womb-like and dreamy.

Susan didn't say much until she pulled into the drive of her new house on Club Lane. She'd been living there since she'd left Michael and sold the Craftsman in Santa Monica Canyon.

I tried calling him on his cell.

What?

His cell phone. I've tried to call him, but he won't answer.

And he won't come to the door?

He locked himself in.

When was the last time you heard him?

Two days before I called you.

Three days ago? Three days?

I heard him moving around. After I called you.

Then she leaned into the steering wheel and sobbed. I held her tight as you can hold a woman when she's breaking up at the steering wheel of a BMW. Touching her always grounded me. Made me feel solid. Real. Her scent. The warmth of her skin. The taste of her mouth.

We could have been something but there was too much history to overcome. After she stopped crying, I hauled her out of the car and into the house. She led me down a long black granite hallway to a white oak door. She pointed.

There, she said. She hung back like it was a plague room and didn't want to go near it. I did.

You wait here, I said. I kissed her hair that still smelled of perfume and sea salt.

***

The door was locked. I knocked. No answer. I kicked it in. Susan screamed. I looked at her and she turned her back and walked away.

The room was dark. Curtains pulled so tight the light had to squeeze its way onto the floor.

I stood for a minute to let my eyes calm down and then I saw him on the bed, naked except for a very brief pair of designer shorts. The kind of shorts a man with hips and a big package can't wear. He lay on his side, one arm straight out, the other tucked under his head. It was the first time I'd ever seen him.

Jon?

No answer.

I felt his skin. He was cold. Very cold. His cheek was slick as if it had been oiled then covered with talc.

I shook him. His outstretched arm flopped loose and I rolled him onto his back and felt for the pulse I knew wouldn't be there.

I pulled back the curtain to let some light in and I saw that the room was almost bare. The bed, a chair, a cell phone on the chair. A sheet on the bed. A pillow. No clothing. Nothing. No radio, no stereo, no boombox, no game boy. Nothing. It had been stripped clean.

He was so thin he looked like his bones were about to let go and spill all over the bed. On the floor, beside the window, there was a trash can and in the trash can six inches of vomit and blood.

Needle marks tattooed the kid's arms. Red rings of infection circled small yellow pustules on the skin. Streaks of infection. The rot you'd expect to see on the arms of an amphetamine addict.

911 answered and I asked for a van and then the police. I went back out to Susan.

She was sitting in a chair in the sunken living room looking out over the pool and the deck where the agapanthus was in full blue bloom.

She knew. I just looked at her and she cracked like a thin ceramic jug and it all came out but it was silent, the kind of crying you see when all the life has already gone out of a body and you don't have anything left but the dry heaves.

I called. The police. 911.

She got up and walked outside, tripping over the jamb and stumbling out to the pool when I caught her.

What are you doing?

He's 22, she said, just 22.

***

The medics came first, then the police, then the medical examiner.

Are you the boy's father? the policeman asked me.

A friend of the mother, I said.

Okay. You're the one who called?

Yeah, I called.

She gonna be all right? She looks beat. She's the mother, right?

Yeah.

Susan didn't talk, couldn't talk for half a day after they took Jon.

Then, over a double scotch, she said,

He was so thin.

The heavy users don't eat, I said. It's not your fault.

I've let everything go.

You were a good mother.

He was my life, she said.

***

Michael came to the funeral, but he didn't look at Susan. He didn't look at me. After the last rites, he got in his steel gray Porsche and drove away.

I stayed with her until she didn't need me and then I went back to Seattle.

At home the squirrel was still sprawled out on the patio deck. Stiff and hard. Sun-baked squirrel.

A thin ring of fat oozed around his furry body like something had spilled out of him.

The Savage God

We were a closed circle, the four of us—John, me, Jeri, Amanda—sharing a big house on Dwight Way. Our kitchen window looked into the bedroom of the house next door where the left-handed tenant sat naked every morning on the edge of his bed testing a straight razor against the crook of his right arm.

The four of us watched the blade, never finishing our coffee until he stood, cased the razor in what looked like a stainless steel sheath, and laid it on the end table.

Amanda: Not today. He's still thinking about it.

John: He wants it though.

Jeri: Why is he always naked?

Me: Because he doesn't want to make it any messier than it will be.

Amanda: Finish your coffee.

Me: I've read about suicide.

John: Tell us.

Jeri: This is really good coffee this morning, who made   it?

Me: He isn't a suicide.

Jeri: How do you know?

Me: Because he lets us watch.

Jeri: Oh. Should we do something?

Me: The Savage God broods on wings of steel, sings in the blood. The day he decides, he'll close the curtains.

Jeri smelled good after her shower, after we had made love, after she had dried and brushed her hair, after she'd doused her skin with a perfumed lotion.

John made coffee. Amanda burned the toast. I opened a fresh pack of Marlboros.

In the room next door, the tenant sat on the edge of the bed, the blade in his left hand and then he turned his head as a woman's hand clutched at his shoulder. He shook his head. Hard. Then he stood, turned his back to us, and a quiver of silver sliced the air and then he knelt beside the bed.

Jeri: Holy shit, he's killed her.

Amanda: Look.

He then faced us, looked up at us, his left hand smeared with blood, blood streaked across his naked chest, and, while we watched, coffee cups in hand, he raised the blade to his throat and with a single, horrific slash, tore his neck nearly off his body. A gusher of blood splattered onto the window. He lunged forward and dove through the glass, shattering it and sprawling on the concrete driveway between the two houses.

Jeri: Good god.

Amanda: Shit.

John: You said he'd close the curtains.

Amanda: Will somebody call 911? For god's sake?

Jeri made the call. We finished our coffee and then we walked next door. John and I broke into the room.

She was an older woman. Gray hair. Skin as soft looking as a young girl's. A big body and bloody and her breasts flattened over her chest as she lay on the bed, head at a terrible angle, blood still oozing from a gash in her throat, a second rip laid open her belly.

I felt her neck. Just the faintest pulse of a heart pushing out the last beat of its life.

Her hair, a swirling mass of gray, spread out on the pillow, but at the left side, a gush of blood, fresh and red matted the gray.

Bloody sheets. A woman's clothing stacked in neat piles on a hassock at the foot of the bed. A pair of black high heels. A black dress.

On the side table, a diamond ring and a diamond encrusted wrist watch.

A bottle of champagne.

Two glasses. An ashtray stuffed with longish filter-tipped English cigarettes.

And beside the ashtray the stainless steel case for the razor. Amanda remained stunned in the hallway. Jeri, closer to the body, covered her mouth with her hand and gasped and gasped again.

Both stepped aside for the man in blue who arrived making a lot of noise. He carried a large revolver in a tan holster on his left side and you saw that he was serious by the size of his forearms. Large forearms. A very large man

Policeman: So you all witnessed this?

Me: Yes, sir.

Policeman: And you didn't try to stop him?

John: No, sir.

Policeman: Why didn't you?

John: This is Berkeley. There are a lot of Nihilists here.

Policeman: Nihilists? What's wrong with you people?

Me: We didn't know today would be the day.

Policeman: You've got a murder slash suicide here you Nietzschean Existentialist numbskull. Have you ever seen a dead body?

Me: No, sir.

Policeman: Not pretty, is it?

John: Who is she? The woman.

The Policeman wrinkled that huge blood hound nose and stretched the way a very large walrus about to mate with a young female might stretch. He picked up a photograph from the night-table, a photo of the dead man and the woman on the bed. The photo was signed—To Mom, Much Love, Gordon.

John: His mother?

Me: Jesus Christ.

Policeman: His mother.

He finished his stretch.

Policeman: You all coulda stopped this.

John: His mother?

Policeman: They'd had this place for over a year.

Me: Is there a note? How do you know it's his mother?

Policeman: A note? Christ. You saw it, right? When does this guy have time to write a note?

John: His mother....

Policeman: I tell you, this stinking town gets weirder every stinking day.

The next morning, when I got up, someone had closed the kitchen curtains.

Amanda: Who do you think will want to live there now?

Jeri: They'll paint it. Won't they? They'll have to paint it.

We drank our coffee and smoked our Marlboros in silence until it was time to go to work.

She Didn't Mean to Do It
She Did Mean to Do It
A Story In Verse for Two Voices with Chorus

She didn't mean to do it.
> A. Alvarez
> The Savage God

She didn't mean to kill herself.
It just happened?
The baby sitter was supposed to be there at nine-
thirty,
but she came at ten.
The note said, Call Dr. X. This is his number.
She didn't mean to kill herself.
She set out clean clothes for the children.
Baked cookies.
Got dressed.
Then stuck her head in the oven
and turned on the gas.
She meant it. She meant to kill herself.

No. It was an obsession
a ritual she acted out once every ten years.

This was the year she was to come back?
A dead woman come back from the grave?

She stuck her head in the oven.

But she didn't mean to kill herself.
On the street, the baby sitter rang. And waited.
Rang and paced.
And waited.
Rang the Super's bell
Rang and knocked.
But the gas, heavy as lead
in Water, drifted down to drug the sleeping super who didn't stir.
All because the Baby sitter came too late?

TOGETHER WITH EMPHASIS
(BLACK VOICE) **She**…..didn't mean…..**to kill**…..
herself.
(RED VOICE) **She**…..**DID**   mean…**to   kill**……
herself.
The baby sitter called the police.
Mrs Hughes has breathed the gas.
Mrs Hughes is in the oven.
You can save her.
She didn't mean to kill herself.

She switched on the gas?
She did switch on the gas
She meant it.
She didn't mean to kill herself.
She didn't leave a note. DIDN'T ….LEAVE…
She left a ….NOTE
A…..SUICIDE…. NOTE

CHORUS

It was a good year.

A rich year.

A year thick with poems that sang psalms to the Savage God.

Odes.... to the Savage.... **God**.

It was a good year,

a rich year,

a thick rich year heavy with poems

bare whispers across the page.

Blood should be enough, she wrote, but you wanted my bones.

She meant to kill herself in this thick rich year laden with ripe rich rimes, images cast in gold.

It was a miracle year

Her year.

Her last year.

The year she stuck her head in the oven and flicked on the gas.

ANNUS MIRABILIS

She's sucked the gas, the baby sitter raved, oh my god.

The gas happy Super stumbled upstairs bleary eyed,

What's she got herself into this time?

Into the oven and sucked up the gas.

It was the year of HER Savage God.

He.... waits...in....the.... corner

beside the knife,

beside the gas knob,

beside the poison bottle.

He waits.

No….No…She didn't mean it.

She did mean it.
She dreamed the sharp edges of razors
sank into the epidermis
plowed into the dermis
slit the fatty layer of her too adipose ugly thick body
sank down to blood.

She did not mean to kill herself.
She wanted to leak a little
She wanted to see it come BIDDEN, the blood,
Begged for, blood breaking the skin willful.
She measured a pint of blood,
watched it seep into a glass—thick, red blood,
thick red blood.

In the black place of her light not shining
she made a mess.
Don't make a mess, her mother said.
Don't make a mess.
She did mean to kill herself.
She swallowed poison pills.
She sucked up the gas.
No matter what.
No matter what.

CHORUS
The Baby sitter came too late.
The Super slept too late.
Who's to blame? Who's to blame?
It will always be too late,

The Little Hand's stuck between 9 and 10.

(Here the Black Voice wails high then decrescendo)
NOOOOOooooooooooooo!!!!!

TOGETHER in a CHANT
BLACK VOICE Always and already and forever.
RED VOICE   STUCK   STUCK   STUCK
CHORUS   Dead   Dead   Dead

She didn't mean it.
Practice? Small incisions, hesitation marks, practice
for the main event.
Death comes in threes. One. Two....
In threes.
The Savage God asks for tribute.
He asks for blood.
He only asks for blood.
She thought her blood would be enough
but he wanted bones.
I am....
The blade
I was....
The rope.
I will be....
......The poison.
She didn't want to be a corpse.
She didn't want to be a corpse?

CHORUS
He anesthetized her.
The Savage God anesthetized her,

He lay her down to sleep.
The Savage God, he's to blame.

Who stuck her head in the oven?
She did… but she didn't mean it.
Why do it? The head in the oven?
No.
To kill herself.
No.

CHORUS
In the Stone Cities, they burned blood.
It rose up in smoke a snake.
They burned it to him.
The Savage God.

She didn't burn blood to him.
No, but she did stick her head in the oven
and flip on the gas. You see….
You don't see….She didn't want to die.
But now it's too late.
Yes, the Baby sitter came too late….
The Super slept too late….

RED VOICE (soft, taunting)
too late.
BLACK VOICE (softer)
no.
RED VOICE (very soft)
too late….
BLACK VOICE (even softer)
no
RED VOICE (fading)

too late...
BLACK VOICE (fading out)
Blame Mr. Hughes...
CHORUS
TOO LATE......

The Tear Garden

Never open the door unless you know who's there.

All my life I've been afraid of that—opening the door to let the infections and diseases and craziness in but I opened the door that morning, a Saturday morning. Wet and chilly. I should have stayed in bed but these days I can't sleep past 4:30, so I was up, working, turning pure, white unblemished paper into black-inked hope—I'm a writer waiting for insight, purpose, anything to lift my morning anguish into art. Dante wrote my biography. It's all there.

I opened the door.

Larry stood on the front step dripping. He looked like a huge wet dog. His eyes were red circles of shame and apology and his mouth quivered and he looked at me with his huge dog eyes and shuddered.

She's dead, he said.

What?

She's dead.

He heaved a sigh.

She wanted you to have this. He shoved an envelope at me. It was a long white thing stained with rain and running blue ink. Under the smear she had written my name. Jack. It spilled across the paper like blood.

Hey, I called. But Larry was halfway down the block. It was then I noticed his bare feet. Wet. A huge man with a bald head wearing a white T-shirt and ragged jeans and walking barefoot in the rain. Hey, wait. But he turned the corner. I heard a car start.

I closed the door.

Flicked the envelope. It was heavy. Wet.

I sat down at my desk, looked at the computer screen where a few lines looked back at me—my shame—and then I studied the envelope. It was heavy. Thick and heavy and wet. It weighed a ton. Too heavy for a human being to handle.

It takes a long time to open an envelope that heavy. I pried at it, slipped a fingernail under the flap, but I was weak all of a sudden and I couldn't open it. It acted like it was made out of some kind of unbreakable paper and had been sealed with some kind of miracle glue. It didn't want to open it.

I took a deep breath. I knew what it said.

Some things you know without being told.

Okay. She'd told me a hundred times before in letters, over the phone, once even e-mail that came like a lightning bolt because I knew she was desperate to send it. She was in pain.

Her own kind of existential pain. Pain that wrapped her up and tied her down and squeezed her until she took pills and then fainted.

That envelope.

Like a stone tablet.

Heavy and wet.

Son of a bitch.

She just dropped it on me, a rock, a brick, a piano, a landslide.

I got up from the desk and opened the door. But Larry was still gone.

No choice then.

Open it.

In the kitchen, over fresh coffee, I slid a knife into the belly of the bleeding envelope, slit it open, laid it open the way a hunter guts a downed deer. Inside there was a letter. I felt the weight all right.

She was talking to me.

So heavy, Jack, she once said over the phone. She called from in Las Vegas after a lost weekend with a paranoid construction equipment salesman named Kent who left her tied up on a bed in a hotel room. I gave him the best blow job he'll ever get, she said, but he was crazy. He thought his wife had followed him. Life is too heavy. I can't even walk, my legs buckle. I'd kill myself, but I'm too weak. Today.

Yes, I said. Oh.

I took a deep breath like a man on the workout bench before he tries to press his weight in steel. I unfolded the letter that was wrapped around a pack of photos.

On top, Sheree. Smiling. In an arbor. She wore a raincoat (white), jeans (washed out blue) and sneakers the color of thunderheads. She was smiling. On the back it said, Me, in Berlin, in the Tear Garden with the other animals....

I broke.

Men break.

I did.

Couldn't hold it back. Some things get you so hard you can't hold them in.

More pictures of her—in Paris. Rome. Budapest. On a bed, smiling.

On a bed with tubes and needles in her arms.

On a sofa wearing a green hospital gown.

A photo of her with her head shaven, her face gaunt and ashen, the color print vivid and in her eyes the hollow place where Thorazine dumps you.

I'd seen her there before. Seen her in drug hell more than once. Eyes dark, hard tunnels driven through hurt running into Limbo.

On the back of that picture, she had written, The Marquis de Sade is my attending physician. I wish you were closer. I can't feel you anymore.

The ink blurred. What? Shit? Blurred and another drop hit her writing and leaked through the blue ink, an army of ants chewed at my eyes spewing wet. God damn it. Sheree. But right then, I couldn't quit crying.

I took a deep breath, set that picture down. Looked at the next photograph.

She sat on a ledge over-looking Tahoe. No other lake is like it. Perfect. The mountains around it are perfect. John Muir said Tahoe was where god, a god, some god got the idea for Paradise. And she looked perfect there. Mountain and lake and woman. One.

On the back, she had written, I'll die here before I go back to hell, Jack. Don't let me go back to hell. Help.

The photos weighed like steel bars on my chest. So heavy I felt them bust my gut, rupture my spleen, spill acid on the world, on the bed, on the floor. I couldn't move.

The last picture was the coroner's photo of Sheree on a gurney, her hair cropped like a convict's is cropped, her skin wrinkled and bleached white as if someone had tortured her. Who took that? Larry?

Oh, she was so beautiful. So tall. So thin. So perfect.

And there she lay in ruins. A temple brought down.

In the morning, I read the letter.

It was from Larry.

Written on a typewriter with overstrikes and typos and odd spacing the way a man will type when he's in pain and doesn't care anymore.

Oh, he wrote. I don't know how she got away. I don't, but I got a call from her at Tahoe. She said goodbye.

She cut her hair off and mailed it to me and then she rented a boat, Jack, and she wrapped herself in her winter coat and rowed out to the middle of Tahoe and she ate every barbie she had saved for the past year going back to her stay in Sonoma, and then she rolled into the water and the coat weighed her down and the pills made her weary. Oh god, what will I do now? Larry.

***

It took a week, but I tracked him down. Found him in a hotel on Skid Road in Old Sacramento holed up like a hermit and so drunk he couldn't talk, so weak he didn't want to. I called the medics, but he died of alcohol poisoning in Sac County. The ME said, He didn't want to live. There was no reason to die. I've brought'em back from deeper down than he was.

Yeah, I said, he just lost his wife.

Ah, he said, sometimes that'll do it. In India they do that, but it's the other way around.

I'm sure he wasn't thinking about India, I said.

Are you responsible for the body? he asked me.

Words brought her back. Got her to breathe, to feel, to live. Put the hair back on her head and got her dressed—in black and white—words as black as her hair had been, white as her teeth had been—and she breathed and walked and talked through Paris and Budapest and

San Francisco, her long legs eating the hills, her smile rich as farmland sunshine. Three hundred pages of her, everything I remembered about here.

An envelope arrived when I was in the second rewrite of *The Tear Garden*. Three hundred pages. It was like she sat beside me giving me dictation.

The envelope came special delivery from a lawyer in Sacramento. A thin white little wisp of an envelope. I opened it.

I found locks of hair. Black hair. But it wasn't the long streams of hair that she twisted around her fingers when she was drinking screwdrivers and smoking long filtered cigarettes as she seduced some guy she'd picked up in a bar. This was her black kinked hair that too many men had seen and tasted and got hung up in their teeth.

Her note was simple. Remember me? She had written it on a slip of paper no bigger than a fortune cookie strip. She'd signed it. Love, Your Sheree.

Tattoo

From the left bank of the Kings River you looked out on the vineyards in the river bottom where the flood water had risen and lapped away the top soil. The vines stuck up like sick men, arms wired together, posts angled and rotting as if the whole world were going to fall apart, bones and all.

Shit, Linard said.

What? I asked.

Church key's broke.

He held up the half quart of Miller. In his hand it looked like a metal worm—shiny, glittery, intact.

How's a guy 'sposed to get stoned...

Linard hurled the broken church key into the river and then jammed his hand into his pants pocket, came out with his pocket knife and with a flick of a wrist snapped out a blade, punched two holes in the half quart and handed it to me.

Don't need no god damn church key, he said.

What's eating you? I asked.

Nothing, Linard said. He punched holes in another half quart, shot the knife blade back home, then, raising the can, guzzled, head back, until he slammed the can down on the ground. Sucker's empty now, he said. Beat that.

Okay, I said, and I lifted my can, poured the cold beer down an open throat the way Linard had taught me and then, when I was about to blow up, slammed the can to the ground. Linard laughed.

Candy-ass. My granny can knock one back faster than that, he said.

Now tell me what's eating you.

Nothing.

Tell me, I said. You told me about the fungus and you told me about Alice Rodriguez. What can't you tell me?

Heart, he said.

Heart?

My heart, he said. He squirmed up on the hood of the Merc, hung his head, shoulders bowed in a way I'd never seen him slouch. And when he looked up at me, there were tears in his eyes.

What about your heart, Linard?

The Corps.

The Corps.

The Corps. He crumbled then and sobbed. White T-shirt shimmering, head bobbing, hands over his face.

Linard Pope crying was like seeing John Wayne in a tutu—improbable, not likely, impossible, no way.

Linard?

I can't join, man, he said. I'm screwed. I tell you.

What are you talking about?

I got a heart murmur, he said. Doc told me I can't join 'cause I got this heart murmur and they can't fix it and I got to tell my old man.

Jesus.

He stood, dust rising in a thin cloud around his feet and he kicked the empty half quart off the bank. It sailed out and arched down and fluttered like a dead metal bird into the brown flow of the river where it bobbed up and down for a few yards then sank. The metal top with its

102

twin holes looked like the face of a drowning man. And then it disappeared.

What're you gonna do?

All my brothers been Marines, he said. My Daddy was a Marine, my Uncles all been Marines and I can't be a Marine 'cause something ate my heart.

Join the Army, I said. The Navy.

Screw you man, he said, you don't understand. What am I gonna do?

What do you think you oughta do?

Linard walked around to the rear end of the Merc, opened the trunk. The Merc was black, shiny black and waxed to a mirror sheen that took the afternoon sun and shot it out in hot eye-searing bolts. From the trunk, he lifted a small black box and from the box he hefted his .38.

I'm gonna kill myself, he said. I'm dead anyway so no sense in sucking up any more water if I'm a dead man.

Okay, I said.

What do you mean Okay?

I mean Okay. I can see you killing yourself 'cause of that, and if you kill yourself can I have your Merc?

Beast, you numbskull.

No, come on Linard. If you're dead what good's the Merc gonna do you?

You piece of crap, he said.

Look. I never knew anybody who killed himself.

Damn you.

What? It's a good vehicle. You die, they'll just sell it to one of those Kingsburg Swedes who'll rip off the header plugs and turn it into a mama's car.

You think? Linard said. I didn't think of that.

He caressed the sleek black rear end of the Merc.

So, I said, what's your decision?

I ain't made one yet.

Sign the pink slip over to me before you shoot yourself in the head, okay?

I'm thinking, he said.

He laid the .38 back in the trunk, traipsed around to the hood, yanked another half quart of Miller from the six pack, punched it open with his frogsticker and sucked at the brew for a very long time. Not a race this time, just a slow guzzling of that cold beer—before he let up, took a deep breath, and looked at me standing back at the other end of the Merc.

You'd let me do it? He said.

Hey, I really want this Merc, man, and if the only way I can get it is if you blow your stupid Okie brains out, well...

He glared at me. Squinted. Then he swilled some more Miller and said,

You don't want me to do it, do you?

If you do, sign the pink slip.

Linard flung the half quart of Miller out and into the Kings River and he returned to the trunk where he replaced the .38 in its carrying case and he slammed the trunk.

You don't know what it means, he said. Now I can't get the tattoo.

Jesus, Linard.

Semper Fi. Every man in my family has Semper Fi on his right arm, man and I go and bust the string.

So you're gonna do what? I asked.

Right now I'm gonna drink another brew, he said, and then I'm gonna go tell my Daddy.

So you're not gonna kill yourself?

No.

You're a selfish shit, Linard, you know that?

Yeah, he said. But what the hell. No Kingsburg Swede's getting this crate.

We sat on the Merc, polished off the six pack until the buzz sang like a hive of bees in my brain and then Linard fired up the Merc and we rolled over the ruts and gullies of the river bank road down to Tulare Street and out onto Sanger Boulevard.

I guess nothing means nothing anymore does it? He said.

I guess, I replied. I don't know.

Yard Work

My yard is overgrown at this time of year. I let it go, let the calendulas go to seed, leave the euphorbia pods to dry on the stem, let the oat grass seed and fly.

I don't call it a garden. It's a yard. Wild and open and crazy. After Laura died, I quit trying to keep nature in order. You can't. You can for a while, but then, you look away for one minute and it runs on you.

The last two weeks of August I clear out the dead things. Strip down to shorts and a T, a pair of sandals, a straw hat, take the morning sun, weed cutter in hand, and clear it out. No mercy.

Next door, in the blue house with white trim, the woman, Kim, watches me. She rocks her baby, Micaela, in her arms. Her garden is manicured, neat, ordered. Hydrangeas bloom the color of aquamarine stones. Before the baby was born, she planted geraniums in pots, window box dahlias, pansies, all bright and sunny. She worked her garden every day.

But now, after the baby, there is a blank look in Kim's eyes as she watches me dig into the dirt. Rocking Micaela, she stands quiet, and then she goes inside. She never says goodbye. She disappears. I hear the door close. Then music comes on. Piano music, new age music, John Tesh. No body. No form. No content. Just notes.

The sun is hot on August mornings. Very hot. I need to clear the yard now or it will be a tangle in the Spring. I like the sun, like to feel the sweat roll off me, like the taste of dust as it boils off the dry leaves with the slight breeze from a sudden movement.

In those quiet moments when no planes fly over head, and for a span of a few seconds freeway noise dips to zero, no cars on the street, no birds, I clip a columbine stem and the hard dark little seeds shower down on dry leaves with a rattle. It reminds me of quiet rain.

In November, when the rains do come, I'll stay inside. I'll write more then. I look forward to November, the dead time, when Irish moss perks up again, when it flowers its small white blossoms, star drops against the magic green. Then rain.

It is late afternoon before I reach the timbers at the edge of the yard. They are rotten now. I set them in while Laura was still here. They are eaten from the ground up—a world of live and die there in the wood. I lift a rotting hunk of hemlock, expose a black worm beetle in full attack. Its mandible scissor sharp, it kills the earthworm, one of the red one that tunnel in the compost, a worm four times the beetle's length. The black beetle has locked into the worm's side like a lamprey on a lake trout where it chews a hole in the side and the worm bleeds until the beetle gnaws it in half. Rotting timbers cover a hidden world. I'll replace them in September before the November rains.

I look up at the sun filtering through the branches of the grand fir that stands between the edge of the yard and the sidewalk. It was a Christmas tree in a clay planter the first year Laura and I lived in the house, the first year, our first good year. I planted it there, watched it grow, bought a deep root feeder to keep it strong and healthy. As it grew, things soured between Laura and me, and then, one day, I found her dead. I don't know why I didn't move out. Maybe in a few years.

Kim and Scott moved in next door the next year.

You're a writer? Kim asked me. What does your wife do?

My wife committed suicide.

Oh, she said. Kim was a tall woman, very Nordic, with chestnut hair and skin that, before she got pregnant, glowed with a rare healthy sheen. Even eight months into her pregnancy, she was slender. Like a very fit animal, she carried the baby high.

We talked, at first, in monosyllables, once or twice a week. Then, just after she found that she was pregnant, and before I mowed the grass, while I weeded and watered and planted, she'd stand on the threshold between the houses and talk to me about plants and when was the best time to seed calendulas and how often did I dig up my tulips, but, after Micaela came, she stayed inside and we talked very little and then she fell into silent watching from her back porch, baby in arms, just watching me.

I'm a good neighbor. A lousy husband, a terrible friend to the three women I've brought to the house since Laura died, but I'm a good neighbor. I mind my own business, make very little noise late at night, and mow the grass once a week.

After Micaela was born, I never mowed the grass until I'd checked with Kim. My habit was to knock, ask about the baby. Last week, when I came, Kim answered. She didn't look well. Dark eyes shadowed from lack of sleep. She held the baby.

I see she's not sleeping, I said.

She never sleeps, Kim said.

Well, I said. Babies get colic.

She's not colicky. I don't know what's wrong.

Well, I'll go cut the grass then.

Scott's left me.

Oh, I said.

He couldn't put up with her crying.

I'm sorry.

I don't know what I'm going to do.

If I can help, let me know.

I wonder if you'll help me unscrew the hose from the back yard, she said.

Glad to, I say. Where do you want it?

On the patio. Out of the way. Beside the door.

I ran the noise maker between the houses, mulching because the City wants us to compost grass clippings. And then I put the mower away. That was last week.

Now, as I pull up chunks of rotten timbers at the edge, stuff a broken piece into the bin, and drag the bin around to the side with the others that are full to overflowing, I look next door. It is quiet, very quiet. Micaela must be sleeping. But it is the depth of the quiet that bothers me. No music. No John Tesh. No piano. Huh. Unusual.

I take a minute to listen. I feel sweat trickle down my back, cooling.

Later, just before the sun sets, I roll out the mower, check the gas, check the oil, then I go next door to ask permission. I don't want to make any trouble. If the baby's asleep, I'll wait. I knock.

No answer. I knock again. Nothing. I haven't seen Kim all day. Maybe Scott came back and they moved out. Or maybe she moved in with her mother.

From the front porch, I peer into the living room. It is a clean room, very neat and tidy. Baby toys. A walker. A baby pack. Pink clothing. A yellow duck mobile dangles from a rod in front of the high chair.

And then, I smell the gas.

Last week the gas company came to our street to lay new pipe. They tore up the sidewalk, dug trenches, fitted every house on the block with new leads, and then filled the trenches and buried the pipes and covered the holes with concrete.

I knock again.

Kim? No answer.

Maybe she's asleep. Maybe the baby went to sleep and Kim fell exhausted. I can wait. Mowing isn't something I like to do, it's something I have to do.

Back in the kitchen, I pour a glass of iced tea, sweeten it, still think about Kim and the baby.

I finish my tea head next door again. Back porch. The sliding glass door is closed. I knock. Smell the gas. It is thick. Very thick.

Jesus. I slide the door open. Inside, the gas smell is thick, so thick I can taste it, so thick I gag on it, so thick I'm dizzy before I take two steps to the kitchen where a garden hose is clamped to a funnel resting over the gas burner on the stove and all four knobs are on full bore and the oven door is open and the knob is on full.

I shut off the gas, open all the doors, slide back the windows, pushing aside a baby bottle full of formula that falls the sink, cracks, and then, holding my breath, I stumble through the house. In the bathroom, in the tub, Kim lies on her back the baby strapped to her belly. They are both livid, flushed, bright red. I snatch up the baby and carry her outside, lay her on the grass then return for

Kim. She is a big woman. A heavy woman. I can't lift her out of the tub, so I drag her through the house, down the hall, to the yard, to the grass and lay her beside the baby, and then I dash back into the house to call 911.

Outside Kim lies limp beside her small, limp child.

The fire truck first, then Medic One and two police cars, and there are a dozen capable anxious men working like ants doing what they have been trained to do, but there is nothing they can do.

Are you the husband? A policeman asks me.

Neighbor, I say.

You found her?

Yes.

Do you know the husband?

Scott, I say, but I don't think he lives here and I don't know where he works. I don't know anything about him.

She's dead, the policeman says.

And the baby?

It's a double, he says..

A Woman of Means
a triptych

1 Sight Reading

She was a woman of means. A woman of sub-stance. When you meet a woman like that you do a gut check on your manhood because she'll chew your legs off then eat you alive.

No. Wait. I don't want to make her sound like a crocodile. I don't want to make her sound like a bitch goddess with fangs and black hair.

She had black hair. But no fangs. She was short. Olive skinned. To see her you didn't see anything special or spectacular—that's how she fit in. But then, you step back, take a second look and you see that the nails are done. Manicured. Painted. You see lips shaped like the small arches in a cathedral. You see clear olive skin clean and with depth. Some women have shallow skin, skin that stretches transparent over the bone, but her skin was a work of art. Any painter would want to spread oils on it, any sculptor touch it with his fingers to make sure it was real.

And the hair.

Thick hair.

Black thick hair with a streak of silver off the left temple. By design.

Hair that cost more to keep up than my car.

And then, after all that, after you work down to the body coated with cloth so fine you know it's handmade, you come to the feet.

Feet can't be built. They're born. Like writers or mathematicians who come with everything right from day one, her feet were delicate little things. Short toenails painted deep scarlet—not chipped. Open toed shoes the first time we met. Feet uncovered, she was more naked than most women in bikinis.

I don't have a foot fetish, but I know men who do and it was easy to see her with a trail of mouth-breathers behind her as she shopped in a store. With those feet, anything is possible.

So, she's not a bitch goddess with fangs, but a fine polished jewel, maybe even a princess.

A woman like that is never taken.

You don't take her.

She doesn't have a history. She just is.

She meets you at a cross roads and you are taken.

She decides. Natural law. You are chosen. She chooses you.

Let me tell you how it feels to be chosen.

She looked at me, eyes wide, lips pursed, hands on the table.

Nothing is said. No words. Just the eyes peeling away years of hesitation and hurt. And then, she stands, the twist of her shoulders says 'you'll do in a pinch, but you're not reproductive material, just a toy', and she wraps the coat of many colors around her and turns and you follow. There's no choice for you. You are the chosen.

Her eyes had the wisdom of a species that knows about prey and her hips talked body language sunlight clear and her mouth, pursed and silent as she looked back at me, deferred to the eyes and I followed.

She lived in a million dollars on the thirteenth floor of a pile of million dollar caves with windows.

You've seen them. High up so your feet don't touch mud, insulated so your silence is absolute.

Glass and steel and silk and marble and wood—textured into objects they take for granted, objects you see later in museums, or in the finer shops so expensive there are no price tags on them.

Her bed was a work of art. Wooden. Carved. Griffins. Acanthus leaves. Trees. Like the lair of a sylvan siren, all wood and flowers and cool, her bedroom, with music—middle eastern music, a kind of church music from the first Christian nation in a language I didn't understand.

Her skin soft as a cloud.

Her hand in mine.

She was alone.

You live by yourself?

No, but he travels a lot.

Oh.

It was the first masculine pronoun of the evening and it shook me. Hard.

Where is he now? I asked her.

She smiled, sat down with apricot nectar in a cut glass tumbler. She laughed.

Are you worried?

Well, kind of.

She touched me then. Her hand on mine. It was the kind of touch you associate with butterflies. Gentle, almost not there, but real, pure, and very intentional—the way she liked to have her breasts touched. Her nipples stroked. Just the tips of the nipples, like a butterfly landing on a flower.

Don't think about me the way you think about other people, women, she said. Ordinary.

Okay, I said. But I've never been here before. I have to play it by ear. Sight read. I don't have a map.

Sight read, she said.

Which fork? I asked.

I'm sorry? She looked surprised, and that surprised me. A woman like that is never surprised.

Is this the main dish or dessert? I asked.

She laughed again. Cascades of quiet like the trickle of water from the miniature waterfall set in front of the Japanese screen with its peonies.

Well, she said, I'm not sure. Do I look like dessert or the entrée?

You're meaty enough to be the main course, I said.

She touched me again. But this time she took my hand and placed it on her thigh, slid me up under the black silk folds of her dress to a very wet place and she closed her eyes and while I swam in her wetness, she let her fingers travel from hand to arm to neck to face and when she opened her eyes she was panting.

Playing by ear, she whispered.

Why me? I asked her.

Oh. What a question.

I mean it, why me?

She shuddered then, my hand wet, slippery, and she grunted.

Because you have small hands, she said.

Small hands. I'm not quite sure what you mean.

I'm not an ordinary woman, she said.

I feel that, I said.

No, I mean my tastes aren't the usual tastes and I don't like men who think that I'm just a woman like every other woman.

She pressed her thighs together then, and, from her throat a guttural cry. Deeper, she whispered, and gently, gently.

Time stopped when I was with her. I looked at my watch and it was nine-thirty and then again and it was eleven and a few minutes later it was after midnight.

On the sofa, legs spread wide, her wetness. I told her that. Time just didn't work there the way it did everywhere else in the universe.

I know, she said. I don't wear a watch.

What do you do if you have to be someplace on time?

Where would that be? she asked.

Well, those toenails. And the masseuse who works that skin to keep it so soft. And the one who waxes your pubic hair.

Oh. That. Well, I just go.

I'm married to time, I said. I can't live without a clock.

Can you learn?

I suppose.

Then take it off, she said.

I think it's grown to my wrist.

And then she set my hand on her lap and unhooked my band and dropped it on the floor. There, she said. Feel lighter?

116

2 Playing by Ear

Love makes you do some crazy shit. I'm not immune. Like the day she took me to the Kingfish Café for lunch.

She was a woman who looked at the little things. Like the bread in her sandwich. Swirls of brown in a lighter brown bread.

Isn't it pretty? she said as she picked at it with her fingers.

Love. Makes you do some crazy shit.

She wore black that day.

An ankle length black dress slit up the side. It's a cheomsung, she said when I asked her about it. From Tianjin.

Tianjin? China?

She looked at me, smiled, held me in those terrible black eyes until I melted and died and then she let me go—the way a predator releases its prey once it knows the outcome. She then picked at the swirled bread with two finger nails the color of salmon roe and she said, He took me to China.

Oh, I said, still not breathing deep as I pulled back from the precipice.

When she talked about herself she was all fire and words rolled out of her but when He came up, she turned into a sphinx.

The diamond on her left hand said He wasn't a temporary arrangement, and the million dollar flat with

117

its Sound view wasn't a toss off gift to someone He didn't care about.

When were you in China?

I bought a dozen of them, she said. She picked at the bread, tasting it the way a gourmet samples wine with deliberate steps. A dozen, she said—red and black, yellow, green, and a sky blue one and one with red peonies and dragons.

Okay, I said.

She let out a long sigh. I wrote him a letter, she said.

I took a bite of the tomato and bacon sandwich with its swirled bread. Bread I'd have eaten without a thought if she hadn't picked at it. Bread that, when she looked at it, somehow turned into a work of art.

We want to split a sandwich, I had told the waiter. He was a tall thin black man with ringlets and a T-shirt that said Boston College on it.

Sure, he said, you want fries or Cole slaw?

I had looked at her. She raised her eyebrows—the prettiest eyebrows over the boldest black and terrible eyes and I forgot the question. What?

He said, Fries or Cole slaw with the BLT split?

All I could think about was the color of her skin where the cheomsung split over her leg and how, in the car, she had rested her hand on mine then brought it to her leg and its heat.

She laughed. Cole slaw will be fine, she said.

I'm sorry, I said when the waiter left. Time stops, my brain quits working when I see your skin in a certain light.

She touched my hand on the table.

Still sight reading? she asked.

And I don't have a road map for this trip, I told her, it's uncharted territory for me. He's been where I've never traveled and I don't know the terrain and I'm not sure I like following in his footsteps.

Um, she said. Her hand was warm. I felt the hard platinum of the diamond ring.

What did you say to him?

What?

In your letter. What did you say to him?

It doesn't matter, she said.

I think it does. I need some direction here.

Is that what you want? Direction? she asked. I looked at her. Saw the first tear form like a small jewel in the corner of her eye and then it dripped down her cheek. She licked at it when it touched her mouth.

I'm sorry, she said.

We waited for the sandwich then, and its Cole slaw and two glasses of water with lemon slices in them.

She was quiet for a long time as she picked first at the bacon then at the tomato and plucked out the bacon and set it aside and then stabbed at a chunk of tomato with her fork.

I need to know where this is all going, I said.

Let it find its own path, she said. I don't expect you.... I don't expect anything...from you...nothing...at all.

What?

She dabbed at her mouth with the cloth napkin. A hint of mayonnaise at the corner of her mouth where the tear had touched just before.

I wanted to reach across, lick the spot, but I took a deep breath. Temptation had been eating at me ever since the first time I saw her walking down the Harbor Steps and saw the open toed sandals and the painted toenails and the bare skin of her thigh.

He wants me to come to Southern California, tomorrow, she said.

I thought...

You thought what? she asked.

I didn't think...I don't know...My brain's dead.

There's a lot you don't know.

There're things I want to say to you that I can't say here with all these people around.

You don't know them, she said. They don't know you. She paused. I don't know why I let it go this far.

She opened her purse, a small black leather kit with a silver clasp and she spread a fifty dollar bill on the table.

That's too much. A BLT only costs that much in New York.

I like him, she said. I like his hair. A man with ringlets. Maybe I ought to trade you in for a man with ringlets.

She stood then, wrapped the gold shawl over her shoulders and led me out of the Kingfish Café into the cold December afternoon and to her car.

You drive, she said. We sat for ten minutes silent. She stared through the windshield.

Are you going? I asked.

Yes, she said. In the morning. There are people he wants me to meet and he wants to show me a business he's running down there.

What's in the letter? I asked her.

The letter just says what I'll tell him tomorrow.

And that is?

She looked at me. Don't be crazy, she said, right now I need you to be there, solid, not crazy. Don't ask me any more questions.

The cheomsung had split again and her leg glistened under the black silk. I wanted to touch her, I needed to touch her, but I held back. She watched my eyes, then smiled.

You love me, don't you?

I love your bare skin. I love your mouth, but I don't know about the rest of you.

I'm an acquired taste, she said. She took my hand and pressed it under the silk against her bare leg and farther up until my fingers were wet and she sucked in her breath. You better take me home, she said.

I drove with my hand in her. My fingers wet. She breathed in ragged staggered, edgy takes, catching like she was in pain but it wasn't pain and she dug her head into the head rest while my fingers slid in and out of her and she opened her thighs but covered the skin with the black silk.

And then she arched her back and went rigid and I pulled into a parking space next to the curb and sat there stunned until she drew my hand away and covered her legs and said,

Get out.

I'm taking you home, I said, and we're going to make love naked on that sofa in front of that Japanese screen.

Get out of the car, she said. Now.

She leaned across and opened the door.

The cold December air sucked the heat out of the car and it raised goose flesh on my neck.

I got out, turned to face her.

She slid into the driver's seat, closed the door and drove away.

It was a week before I saw her again. A midnight call. Her voice hoarse, dusky, the same voice she used after she made love.

I need to see you, she rasped.

You're back, I said.

I need to see you, she said again.

Tonight? It's twelve fifteen.

If you don't let the battery run down on that watch, she said, I'll break it next time I see you. You're becoming hard to take. Time.

It's midnight, I said, I haven't heard from you in a week and you want me to drop whatever it is I'm doing and come to see you and you know I have work and I do work tomorrow.

You can go to work from here, she said.

What did you tell him?

Are you coming?

No.

Don't be mean, she said. Please.

I need to know some things, I said.

I'll meet you.

When?

Right now.

Are you dressed? I asked her.

No. I'll slip on a coat. I've always wanted to meet a lover naked at night wearing just a coat. Wait in your car at the corner. I'll come there, she said.

3 Road Map

The thing I liked about her was the way she ate with her fingers. The way she broke open a piece of bread to pluck out the soft heart, savor the small crumbs she laid on her tongue.

And then the smile when she saw my eyes on her.

When a woman hooks you with her eyes, you're dead—you know it, she knows it.

She had this way of cutting her meat—taking a piece of steak or a slice of chicken Kiev, and then, holding her fork in her hand picking at the meat skewered on the tines, tasting it, eating it, then licking her fingers. And always the smile.

But, eating with her fingers didn't undo anything. She'd poke at the string beans on her plate then while looking at me, pluck a bean by the end and suck it into her mouth and she'd somehow keep talking and it all looked right, no break of decorum, and of course it drove me crazy.

Insouciant. Insouciance. Not worried. The French have a word for a woman like that. A form of negligence, the way a woman wears a negligee—not worried. She was somewhere else, from somewhere else, another country maybe, a country most of us never see, but a few of us know about when a woman such as that opens the door for you.

Into a world where it was okay, even suggestive, to eat with your fingers.

Ice cream.

She dabbed the tip of her index finger into the dish and raked a glob of chocolate and raised it to her mouth and sometimes, after she'd eaten, a tiny dab of dessert clung to her lips and I always wanted to lick it off. Lick her. Suck her.

You know, I said, something about the way you eat with your fingers.

Erotic, she said, isn't it?

Yes.

You're not the first man to tell me that.

I don't see any other women in here eating with their fingers.

Am I like most women?

Steak. Potatoes. Chicken. Salad. All cut with knife and fork but some of it picked between finger and thumb and plopped into her mouth.

It all changed the day she took me to lunch.

She wore the black cheomsung she wore the first day we made love. The cheomsung is a dress made for her. The cheomsung is a dress a woman can wear with total elegance or with total neglect. In a cheomsung she can look like a princess or a whore. All it takes is a flick of a button and the thigh slit opens and what was hidden is no longer.

The slit in this dress, she said, is appropriate for an infidel, don't you agree?

I don't think of you as an infidel, I said. That's kind of a 50's concept, isn't it?

She laughed.

When you're owned, it's always the 50's, she said.

The restaurant was one of those tiny places you have to know about because there's no sign, no phone, they don't take reservations, and everyone pays cash.

How do you know about this place? I asked her as I sat facing her in candlelight at noon.

He used to bring me here before his divorce, she said.

Oh.

I am what I am, she said.

The waiter came. A tall thin pale man-child with round hips and patrician white androgynous shoulders.

He's been gelded, she said. She took his hand, patted it, smiled at me.

He blushed like he'd never been kissed. He said,

Have you decided?

Salads, she said. Chicken Caesar for me and the artichoke and prosciutto for...my friend.

Once alone, I said, You're joking, aren't you?

About him being gelded?

Yes.

Does that shock you?

Shock me? That he's a gelding? No. Why did you say that?

He's in love with Archer.

Who is Archer?

He owns this restaurant.

What does that have to do with it?

She looked at me. Smiled. Eyes infectious. She said,

How far would you go to please your lover? Would you cut yourself?

Why are we here today?

I need your advice, she said.

I'm not good with advice.

He wants me to go to Paris.

So go.

For a year.

A whole year?

At least.

Well.

I don't want to go, she said. She touched my hand.

Ah. Well. He runs the check book, doesn't he?

Will you come with us?

Us?

The gelding brought our salads. She waved her fork at the plate, then plucked a succulent chunk of chicken breast from a bed of lettuce and popped it into her mouth and then she licked her fingers. She moaned as she sucked the dressing, closed her eyes.

Well, he won't know you're there, she said.

I ate my salad with a fork. She disemboweled a roll and pulled the white center from it and put it in her mouth and chewed it and then she ran her index finger over the pat of butter nearest her and licked her finger then she speared a chunk of lettuce with her fork and bit it and chewed it and then swallowed.

No, I said. I won't.

No? That's a final No or an I'll think about it and let you know tomorrow No?

Final no.

She rose out of her chair then and leaned across the table, her breasts grazing the candle that flickered out and she kissed me on the mouth—lips tasting of roast chicken—I don't want to lose you, she said. She sat back down. Think about it. Paris, together, for a year.

And my job? My house? My life?

She picked at her salad, fingers stirring the lettuce, poking at the pieces then dipping into the dressing and cheese flakes on the rim of her plate. In the half-dark, her skin glowed that hot cherry glow she wore just in the first few minutes after she orgasmed—a glow I had learned to love, a glow I learned to see, a glow that always made me want to go at her again.

Then I thought about not seeing her for a year and the bottom fell out.

Right then I knew I was in love with her. Nothing I could do about it.

I was in love. I didn't want to be in love. Not with her. Not with anyone. Not now. But it was too late.

She looked at me through lowered lashes. Her nostrils flared. I want you to take me home, she whispered, and do things to me.

He'll never know, I'll make sure of it. He'll never know.

Numb

I have an ironclad rule—I walk out of a room, I close the door and I don't look back. The next day it's all new anyway. Everything.

But I found out I can't close the door on smells. Somehow, for some reason, I went back to her that day. Break a rule, you break your string, you die. But I went back.

Smells. On my hands, in my nose, on my clothes. A perfume, a sweet scent like honeysuckle or clover blossom or rose petals crushed. All mixed up in a heady stew of smells—clinging to me like oil on a duck's back.

Maybe that's why I went back.

Maybe that's why I tried the door on the 11th floor.

The smell of her on my hands. Still. I knocked. Waited in the alcove. Then I tapped at the door again. No answer. I tried the handle. She had forgotten to lock it.

I looked around, checked to see if anyone was watching me, then stepped into that room still thick with the scent of sandalwood candles, cinnamon, even a hit of bay.

I stepped inside. Waited. Listening.

Music still on the system. Armenian music. Hovhaness. Polyrhythmic. Music built on modals so old they had names and the crisscross of melody and rhythm matched my heartbeat. I turned it down. Didn't want to turn it off. Waited. Felt out of place, an intruder, without her beside me. And then I heard glass shatter. And a groan. I rushed into the bedroom.

The bed was just as I left it. Pillows on pillows and a blue comforter at the foot of the bed and a blue house robe draped haphazard across the chair where I had left it, and the towel on the bed, yellow, full of her smell and mine mingling, and on the towel spots of her menstrual blood.

Glass breaking.

Music.

Strange counterpoint to the groan. I called her.

No answer.

In the bathroom, she lay in the tub, naked, water sloshing over the side. I shut off the flow, pulled the drain plug, lifted her out expecting to see crimson stained wrists or a groin slit beyond repair but she hung limp in my arms, hot, her skin smelling like rose oil, slick and sweet and smooth and her hair, long black wet tangles clung to her forehead and her head lolled to one side pressed against my chest—now soaking wet—and I carried her back to the bed, laid her down, and shook her.

Her eyes opened. She smiled at me. Then closed them again.

What have you done? I asked her.

Ummm, she muttered. Sleep.

What did you swallow?

I wrapped her in the blue comforter, up to her chin, so she looked like a dark-haired angel in a blue cloud, a pre-Raphaelite creature in death throes.

I ran to the bathroom, found the bottle of Demerol, glass splintered on the floor.

Demerol.

I looked at the prescription on the bottle—twelve tablets. All gone.

Back with her, I rolled her to the edge of the bed and, forcing my fingers into her mouth—so smooth, so wet, so lovely—gagged her. The tablets spewed onto the carpet and she retched and then collapsed, head hanging over the side facing the floor.

We sat for an hour, an hour and a half before she moved, before she rolled over and flopped back, her hair sprayed out against the pillow black wires medusa-like. Even half dead she exuded the primordial urgency that drew me to her a year before. Now, her body said to mine, now...

She looked at me. Eyes flashed.

Why? she asked.

Why what?

You aren't supposed to be here.

Twelve tablets, I said. Twelve. You tell me just what the hell is going on.

She turned away. Head pressed into the pillow. Hiding her face.

My throat, she said.

What?

My throat. Your fingers in my throat. You were harsh.

What if I hadn't come back? I asked.

Why did you?

Why do you think?

I don't know.

Do you want to die? I thought we were through that. You said you'd flushed the Demerol. You lie. Do you want to die?

The numbness, she whispered, I can't feel you in my mouth anymore.

Look, I said, don't do this. I'm calling a doctor.

No. She gripped my hand, glared at me, nails sharper than talons biting into my skin.

I took a deep breath. Let it out. Those nails. On my bare back. Digging in. Jesus.

All right, I said. No doctor on one condition. You tell me what's going through that...I mean...I want to know.

Oh god, she said. She raised my hand to her cheek. Can you feel me?

Yes.

She sighed. I can't feel anything, she said. It's like I'm shutting down. My cheek, my face, my fingers.

It's okay.

No, it's not okay.

I stroked her forehead, fingers laced in those black tangles of hair. She relaxed.

It'll stop, she said, one day you'll touch me and I won't feel it anymore. I'll be dead.

No you won't. There are doctors.

Not for this.

Listen to me. Three hours ago, none of this...you.

You never listen to me, she said.

Okay.

She sat up against the headboard of carved oak, a baroque headboard like something you'd see in a museum, and she stared straight ahead, her hair hanging down over her breasts like Lady Godiva on a horse, her belly almost flat, her thighs muscular and ripe, her feet small, nails painted blood. Then, she looked at me.

I love you, she said. I love the feel of your hands on me, on my skin, in my mouth, in me...Without that, there's nothing worth living for.

Hey, hold on, I said. Don't I have a say?

Do you? she said.

She closed her eyes then and curled up into a tight ball, knees drawn up, head resting on joined hands, feet held tight as if she was afraid she'd come apart. I stroked her thigh, her back, ran a hand up her neck, grasped a tangle of hair in my fingers, and then I leaned down and kissed her nape.

She said, I haven't had a hickey since I was a senior in high school.

Are you hiding any more Demerol?

What?

Any lye? Barbies? Nembutal?

Why?

Where you go, I go, I said, together.

Oh god. No.

I mean it. I don't know why I came back just now. Something. Maybe I smelled death the way a bluebottle fly smells it.

She clenched my hand in hers, held me tight against her. Breathing hard. Then sobbing. Her whole body quaking. I wanted to nuzzle her breasts. Suck her nipples in my mouth. Make her come again. Hard. Again.

You don't mean it, she said.

Oh I do.

You can't mean it.

Never meant anything more, I said. So what do you say? Any more drugs in there?

She released my hand. Sat up.

Do you really love me? Even if I'm numb? Even if I can't feel anything? Even if I can't feel you inside me?

I can feel, I said. You take that, what do I have?

Your story, she said.

What story?

The one about the man, the exile, whose hands were blown off, she said. He hated not being able to feel the skin of his lover.

And I hate it when life imitates art, I said.

Hold me, she whispered. Forever. I want to die with you in me.

I lay beside her, shirt still wet, she still naked, and I locked my legs around her and squeezed.

Do you feel that? I asked.

She nodded. Oh yes. Yes.

Outside, on the street, the sounds of the city clashed in counterpoint to her breathing. The scent of rose oil on her skin wafted up and over me.

Theory of Chaos

I'm a man who disciplines himself. Never do anything unless I've thought it through. I learned this from the women in my life all of whom looked like they were running raw and wild but under the craziness there was order. I just didn't see it.

Discipline for a writer is life and death. I never open the door unless I'm expecting someone. There's a reason for this—Anyone who just drops in either doesn't know I need my time or it's someone who's trying to sell me something and I already have everything I need. Too many times I've opened the door to find bad news jammed up against the threshold like a leech on bare leg.

It was a good day and I was feeling good but it turned sour eight hundred words into a story rewrite. I'm taking it deep, way down past the pain to the place where the bones and meat are two worlds and you see the god of fiction naked and begging you to put a suit on him. When you're down there, you're already a little bit crazy and you forget and so when the doorbell rang I broke the discipline, broke my main and primary and unbreachable rule—I answered the door.

Lu stood there wearing a blue dress spotted with blood red polka dots. She wore black high heels and her mouth quivered as she said, Max. Oh god, Max.

And then she collapsed through the doorway and into my arms. That was Lu. Falling apart.

Two double shots of Jack Daniels later she coughed and gagged and asked did I have a joint.

Okay, I said when she was upright and bright-eyed and the polka dots on the dress had stopped dancing, why are you here?

Kathleen, she said. And then she broke again and bawled until the blue dress was stained with tears.

What about Kate? I asked.

She's dying, Max.

Oh. Where is she?

She went back to Eden.

And Mom let her come back?

She can't say no to Kate. You know that.

And you came here instead of calling because you haven't paid your phone bill for two months.

Hell with this, Max. Those things don't matter. I want you to come back to Eden with me, Max. I can't see her alone.

Mom?

She'll never forgive me, but I've got to see Kate before...

And then she broke out for the third time—tears and wet and sobbing.

I sat with her on an overstuffed leather sofa that soaked up the tears as well as a sponge and I held her hand the way I used to hold her hand when she was coming down or coming back from a binge, her heart in tatters and her virtue splattered all over LA or left on the top of a strip joint Okie bar somewhere in Bakersfield.

I hated what she did to herself. I hated the way she did it, but a little sister is blood and blood has a mystery to it you can't just shut out.

I'd tried to find that mystery in everything I'd written for the last ten years, tried to write it out, to find out why you love the blue eyes and the red hair and the tall thin woman in high heels more if she's your sister.

She came around and wiped at her eyes and the herky-jerky crying stopped and she said, Max, I've made a stinking mess of it, haven't I? I know it. And I don't deserve to have anyone love me anymore, but Kate's going and I've got to be there.

Okay, I said. Let me get some things together.

I packed the writer's essentials—a fifth of Jack D, a pint of Old Overholt twenty-year old rye, a liter of Mexican aguaradiente, two pairs of socks, a pair of Jockey briefs, and my sandals.

You'll need a couple of shirts, Lu said from the doorway. How can you live like this?

Like how?

Like a hermit, like a bum, like a tramp.

I'm not the one who takes it all off in Lola's Cantina, sweetheart, I said. and as soon as I said it, I was sorry. Look, Sis, you know I didn't mean to hurt you.

I know, she said. But it's true. I don't think you'd make much of a hit with that belly of yours.

She laughed. When she laughed it was bells chiming or the sun shining and under the lipstick and the perfume and the blue dress there was a sweet kid, my sister, who'd gone bad one night when she was sixteen and wild and crazy and it just never stopped. She'd call to tell me she knew she'd made a mess of her life. Then she'd ask for a couple hundred bucks to tide her over. I never said no.

Her car was a piece of crap so we took my Beetle.

The new Beetle is a sports car disguised as a toy. Top speed 160. Turbo charged. Five speed transmission.

Spoiler that rises at ninety miles per hour. It hugs corners the way you hug a baby and it glides from sixty to one-ten before you can hit the left turn signal.

Slow down, she said. This ain't the beetle you had in high school.

I'm not the boy I was in high school, I said.

I saw your name on TV, she said. That's big time stuff, brother.

I'll bet you didn't even watch the movie, I said.

No. I fell asleep. You write the most boring shit.

Thanks. I'll remember that.

But Max...

Yeah?

I'm so proud of you. At least you've succeeded at something.

Don't talk crap, babe.

I can't even pay my phone bill on time.

She settled in, got hold of the cornering strap and we hit the Grapevine and turned north and east without any red lights or sirens wailing behind us and we pulled in to Eden at two o'clock in the afternoon. It all looked like it had looked twenty-five years before.

Oh god, Lu said. She sniffled.

I've got a question, Lu, How'd you hear about Kate before I did?

Eileen called me.

Eileen?

Kate's uh, well, Kate, Max, didn't you know?

Know what?

Oh Jesus, this god damned family. Kate's gay.

Kate's gay?

And she's dying, Max, with complications...

Oh shit. But...

I can't explain it, she said.

***

Mom's house was the way it had always been. The box myrtle hedge was bigger and the dirt a little bit dryer and the tile roof built with Mexican red clay had a little more soot on it than it had twenty-five years before, but it was home and by god home is home.

You first, Max, Lu said, you go in first.

***

The house was cool, the way an adobe is in summer, cool and a little bit dry but comfortable.

Kate lay on a low bed in the living room in front of a window where a slice of sunlight cut across her chest. She looked like she'd forgotten to eat for a couple of years. When she looked at me, there was a wildness in her eyes, kind of like a trapped animal and she panted and raised her hand to me and muttered, Maxie, oh Maxie, oh honey and then somehow she started to cry.

I heard Lu behind me and she was bawling like a roped calf and then she sort of crashed to the floor beside the bed and the two of them sobbed and bellered until there was nothing left but the dry heaving of wept out grief.

Where's Mom? Lu asked.

A voice behind me said, She's in town.

I looked up to see a tall thin woman wearing a plaid short sleeved shirt. Her hair was cut into a brush and her face was plain and unpainted. She had on a pair of Birkenstock sandals and baggy jeans.

You're Eileen, I said.

Hi, she said.

Have you had the test? I asked her.

138

She let out a big sigh and she puckered up and covered her mouth with her hand.

I'm afraid to, she said. I don't want to die.

Red

When we were kids, still in high school, John kept a .38 revolver in a black leather holster in the glove box of his Crown Victoria. It was a heavy weapon with crosshatched wooden grips that bit your palm when you squeezed the handle. It smelled of gun oil and gun powder, that sickly sweet stink of the dead.

On Saturday nights, because we didn't know how to do things yet, we drank Jim Beam straight from the bottle and when the whiskey had burned a new path down his throat, he fondled his .38 the way other guys fondled the breasts of sophomore girls hungry for their first orgasm and then, testing the weapon, he placed the barrel in his mouth. His teeth clicked, enamel on steel, and he closed his eyes and closed his lips.

After a minute with taste of death in his mouth, he'd release the barrel from his bite and swallow another mouthful of Jim Beam.

I can see it, he said. It'll be a sunny day in a field. I can see it, really.

Put that thing away, I told him. I don't like it when you play at it. If you're going to do it, do it, but don't play at it.

I'm not playing, Jackson, he said. It's in my blood. It's what I'm born to do.

It's not in your blood.

My granddad shot himself in the mouth with a shotgun, he said. My dad slit his own throat with a razor.

It's not in your blood, I said.

He holstered the .38, tucked it back in the glove box and polished off the pint of Jim Beam.

And then we drove.

Drunk, still high from the taste of death, still wrapped in the warm clutch of Jim Beam, still hungry for the blur of the white line when the Ford howled its 400 horses and blew off the hubs of hell. I remember, later, when I am old, the line from the Epic of Gilgamesh—You have hammered in the gates of hell to feast upon the living.

On Saturday night I never knew if there would be a Sunday morning or if we'd die in the Crown Victoria wrapped around the abutment of the steel bridge over the Kings River.

I never knew.

And that was the thrill. At 95, 100, 105 MPH to take the big curve where River Bottom Road hooked into Church Avenue, down to the water, a long sweeping curve that eased you up and around like you were on a long tether and then flung you down on the flat onto the bridge, threaded you between high concrete abutments lit with yellow lamps like the mouth of purgatory and then the rush when you floored it, red-lined it until the needle lay flat as a dead animal before bouncing back and the rush when you backed off, slowed down, because after the bridge it was all flat and wide and there was only speed and none of the feel of the angel of death breathing down your neck.

And Sunday came every day, but one. The day, twenty-six years later when they found him in his Ford F150 in a field.

I was in Seattle on a trip when Pam called me. I felt my throat catch when she said it. *They found him in his pickup in a field.*

Pam, crying, said it three times... *They found him in his pickup in a field...* like it took that many times for it to work its way through the tears... *They found him in his pickup in a field...*the words falling into holes along the way. Three times to get it all out of her mouth.

The first time I didn't believe it. I didn't want to believe it. By the third time, I knew it was true. It had to be true.

When? I asked her.

Saturday night.

Oh, I said.

He didn't come home from work.

Do you want me to come back down?

Why? There's nothing you can do here.

Is there a service?

No. Nothing. You know how he was.

There ought to be a service, I said.

Who'd come? Everyone will know how he did it, and they won't come.

How did he do it, Pam?

You know.

How can I know?

With a .357, she said. In the mouth.

I'll come down, I said.

No. Don't. I don't want to see you. Not right now. Maybe not ever.

Don't shut me out now.

Why not? she said.

I want to talk to you. I want to be with you.

You're so stupid, she said.

I'm sorry. I don't want to be stupid.

I don't want to see you.

Pam, I said, you mean everything to me.

She laughed. That's not what I mean, she said. I don't care anymore. You never loved me.

She hung up. I heard the tears in her voice.

***

I went back to Bakersfield and I collared the deputy who'd found John. He was a slow man, a big, deliberate man with hollows in his cheeks but with bright eyes that saw everything.

You're a friend of his, he said.

Not a question, a statement. A friend of his.

Yes, sir, I said.

He sure did it up.

Tell me, I said. I need to know.

I've seen maybe half a dozen of these, he said, out like that . Most of them ranchers taking a 12 gauge to it.

What time? I asked.

Two-thirty in the morning. Lights were on. You can see it from the county road so I figure it's a couple of kids getting in trouble, you know, but then I heard the shot.

You heard it?

Oh yeah. Just when I pull up. Doors're open, he's got his legs sticking out, took the magnum in his mouth and most of his head's blown out the passenger side, hardly a drop of blood anywhere but a little on the seat and not much there.

Oh shit, I said.

Never found the bullet. It's out somewhere in the dirt. Oh. And there was a bottle of Jim Beam on the ground, he said.

Jim Beam?

Yeah, a whole fifth. Kentucky Courage. I figure he'd got it all down. You're a friend of his, then.

We were in school together.

Oh yeah, where's that?

Up in Sanger, I said.

I know people in Sanger, he said. Got an uncle up there.

Hmmm, I said. It's growing these days. Too close to Fresno.

Hell's fire, he said, everything's too close to something these days. Getting so a man has to kill himself to get any peace at all.

Yeah, I said. That's the way it is.

***

Pam looked sick. Pale and thin, like she'd forgotten to eat for a month. She wasn't happy to see me. I told her I'd talked to the deputy who found him. I was sitting on the sofa where John had sat for years watching Death Valley Days reruns.

Did he leave a note? I asked her.

She smiled a widow's wan smile and shook her head.

It wasn't because of us, she said.

But he knew.

I don't know if he knew. If you didn't tell him, I didn't.

It wasn't right, I said.

Did you mean even one thing you ever said to me? she asked.

Every word. I meant every word.

She sat silent, tears rolling from those dark eyes.
Then she said, The insurance doesn't want to pay.
They don't on suicides, I said. It's in the fine print.
I didn't even know he'd bought it.
Are you okay? Will you be okay?
No, she said. No, I won't be okay.

Kafka wanted to turn his premature natural death from tuberculosis into artistic suicide by having all his writings destroyed....
                                          A. Alvarez, The Savage God

Ashes

I burned them all. They made a good, hot fire.
Yellow flames tainted with blue fringes.
Tongues of fire. Eating me.

I burned them all—all my writings.
Black ash, the image in the dream. Black.

She came home. She snuggled against me, her hair mussed, glasses hung on a chain around her neck, her bra sticking out of her purse.
Black ashes are all that's left.
Now.

It's a suicide, killing myself through immolation. Burning my pages. All of them.
Why did you do it? she asked me.
Her skin was flushed, her lips chewed raw.
Who was he? I asked her. Did he have a name? Did you orgasm for him?
Why did you do it? She repeated, nestled against me, her heat an aphrodisiac that made me breathe hard, made me want her even knowing what she'd just done. Now you'll have to start all over.

The black ash.

When you burn a lifetime, a few bones stick out of the pyre. A few metatarsals of the poems with no legs. Ribs of still-born novels.

Digits from the stories that grew old and gray on the shelf.

You can live a long time on regret.

You'll regret it, she said.

She yawned.

Did you orgasm for him? I asked again.

I don't want to tell you that, she said.

Why not?

You always act like a jealous freak, she said. I won't tell you.

You did. You said you wouldn't, but you did.

Black ash. A mountain of meat seared black. The first match took hold of the title page of <u>Mister</u>, a fresh novel six hundred pages long, and the flames scorched my face as I shoved chapter after chapter into the fire until its filthy mouth roared back at me like a hungry animal.

She closed her eyes.

You're a slut, I told her.

Ummm, she said.

A malicious, cheap whore.

Oh yes, she snickered. You'll regret it.

I never regret anything, I said.

Nothing? She sat up. Nothing?

The fire ate me, seared my skin, blistered my arms and hands, made me sweat and I imagined Joan of Arc sweating at the stake as I read her poem aloud to fire, the

147

only audience it ever had. It was gone in a trice. A trice. So they say in England. God, I hate England if only because of Shakespeare. How can I be a writer with that specter at my back?

She unbuttoned her Levis, peeled them down to the white, white panties with the red rose at the waist, underwear I gave her on our third anniversary the night she came back smelling of bourbon and sweat and that awful, dreadful stench of another man's sweat on her. She stripped for me, held out her hands to me.

You make me sick, I said.

She kissed me, her mouth still reeking of cigar and bourbon and the fading odor of sex.

Why? I asked her. Why do you do this?

Ashes. Black and ugly. White flakes like the charred corpses of burnt bodies. I burned all of her. The poems to her renewed virginity the first night we made love, the stories of her coming of age as she yielded to me, everyday, the novel about a love that will last forever—all gone.

Her mouth was like cranberry juice.

Her cheeks the color of Rio Oso peaches.

Her neck smooth as rose petals,

Ageless.

But she was a whore who made men crave her the way an addict craves his drug. And she craved them.

Ashes. White, fluttery ashes raining down with the stench of charred skin.

My heart.

My legs.

My hands.

My eyes.

Burnt.

At the end, in the embers, I was empty. Useless. Tired. My whole life gone.

So, she whispered, her leg crossed over mine, are you going to kill yourself now or later?

You have already killed me, I said. I never wanted very much.

You just wanted all of me, she said.

Yes.

You can't have it all, she said. I give away to men I don't even know the thing you want exclusively to be yours.

I kissed her mouth to shut her up.

Ashes.

Boxes of paper.

I'm a collector. I've collected every word I ever wrote. Every page. Every paragraph. Every sentence. Scraps. Whole manuscripts. A hundred stories written and rewritten and rewritten again. I kept it all until it piled up and flowed out like a river and I needed shelves and cabinets to contain it.

This is a reeking mess, she said the first night I brought her home.

She wore a little excuse for a dress and her breasts pushed halfway out of the scoop top of the chemise and her legs looked like a wild animal's—so thin in her high, black heels.

I'm a writer, I told her. I'm messy by nature.

I couldn't live in this filth, she said. Where's the bed? Or do you rut on the floor like an animal?

To me she was a virgin but already she had swallowed half a million anonymous men. Is that what made me love her? Love her? I couldn't live without her. I needed her. To see her. To feel her fill my eyes every morning.

With her in the house, my writing changed. What was hard became easy. Words came like gushing cataracts over a huge waterfall. Nothing was impossible. She was everything I needed, but she needed more.

I tamed her. I wiped off the mascara. I took away the push-up bra and the thong panties and the high heels and replaced them with sensible shoes and sensible cotton panties and a bra that didn't show it all off for any man. And it killed her.

I can't live shut up here like this, she said.

What do you want?

I need to feel hands on me, she said. I need something besides words.

It was our first break. She left me. I mourned. I looked for her. I found her in a bar, her legs crossed, heels high enough to cripple her, and a man beside her feeling her tits through a see-through blouse.

Come home, I said.

Piss off, she told me.

I saved her. Made her come back. But we struck a deal.

She went out.

She did what she wanted.

She came back.

She lay against me, sleeping. I was all right then.

Ashes.

The fire burned something in me the way a bird on a roasting spit turns black. The blackness didn't slough off the way the skin of an overcooked bird will. The blackness had burned down into my bones. I was finished.

I rose. Stretched away from her curled up on the sofa, her sex still stinking of strange men and I didn't dare imagine what she had done to them or how they had abused and tortured her.

I went to my study, that sacred place where I wrote, that crucible where I created flesh and blood and sin and longing.

It had been cleansed by fire. It was bare the way a new house is bare before you move new furniture in, or bare the way a room is when you have grown sick of your own excesses and thrown it all way and haven't yet started over.

On the desk there was nothing but a revolver.

I sat in the swivel chair with the padded arms where I slaved to make her immortal.

You're a fool, she said.

I turned. Looked up. She stood in the doorway naked except for the white panties and sun glasses on the chain around her neck.

You've burned all your books too, she said. You're insane.

Why can't you be just with me? I asked her. It's not much to ask.

She laughed.

I raised the revolver. She gasped. I looked at her and then I shot her in the head. She spilled to the floor. Her legs crumpled under her.

I reached for a box of matches.

I was already dead.
Ashes. Black. Fluttery ashes. Nothing but ashes.

Big Sis

Streetlight filtered through a high window at the end of a hallway. The window was gray with dust and masked with cob webs, tangles of flies and moths, carcasses sucked dry by a spider long gone. It was seven o'clock on a Kansas City Spring evening.

I shuffled down the hallway past newspapers and bottles till I came to the last door on the right. The door was dark blue. Shredded like a cat had clawed the paint. A doorknob flopped loose, holes in the shaft like black blisters in the brass. I would have knocked but the door was unlocked so I poked at it and it swung back silent as a sigh.

Cora was out cold on a bed with no covers, on a mattress with no sheet. She lay curled up, hands tucked between her legs. Her hips were a high mound covered with a black lace slip and her hair spread out on the pillow in an auburn cloud.

It took my breath away.

She breathed through her mouth, lips slack, making a rattling sound. At the corners of her lips spit had caked up like small white chunks of junk or the residue of broken dreams.

A green wooden chair stood by the door. I sat down and took off my gloves and closed my eyes. Street noise rose up like a toxic fog -- horns, voices, car doors

153

slamming, and the sound of kids kicking something, maybe a can, maybe one another.

I was tired. For three weeks I tracked Cora. Tracked her by following the slime she left, like a slug eating its way through the night. Her trail led through Bakersfield to an apartment in Fresno where a woman named Norma threw a telephone book at me, and said that if I ever found her, why didn't I just kill her because she was no good to anybody alive.

In Reno I ran into a hooker named Tamara, a tall strawberry blond with vacant eyes and long fingernails. She gave me a name in Kansas City. With a name, you can thread your way through the rot of a world where sunshine is a dirty word. If you work at night you wear gloves because most of the work is by feel and what you feel you don't want on your skin.

Cora rolled onto her back. Her hair wound under her head, a few strands looping across her face and catching on her white teeth. The ropes of red hair fell over her naked breasts. She curled back into a little ball and tucked her hands under her cheek. Asleep she looked like an angel.

The room was cooling off. In the closet I found a cardboard box full of rags and a beat up tweed bag with a wooden handle. A red wool coat was jammed in the bag

The red coat smelled like mildew. I laid it over Cora then closed the window and as I closed the window I smelled coffee. A cup of coffee. I needed coffee.

The kitchenette was a cabinet with a linoleum countertop that had been worn to a lifeless black. There were stubs where the faucets used to be. No coffee. Nothing to eat. No dishes to eat it on so I went downstairs to a cafe called The Diner. In the night-time bulge that every city grows there's always a Diner. Even junkies have to eat, sometime. I sat looking out the window thinking maybe I should have tied Cora down so she couldn't get away without me seeing her.

The Diner was the kind of place where they keep the sugar under the counter with the ketchup bottles. I bought a roast beef sandwich and two cups of coffee. Then I went back upstairs.

Cora had sprawled out, her left leg hooked over the edge of the mattress, the foot pointing at the coat on the floor. She had long legs and thin ankles. Her thighs had thickened a bit because she didn't swim anymore. Once her legs had been muscular and tanned, but now they were black and blue like someone had hacked at her with a coat hanger. She had a dark blue vine tattooed around her left ankle. Three red roses hung from the vine. Cora's left eye was bruised and her lower lip swollen. I wanted to reach out and brush the bruises away. Oh man.

I watched her sleep. It was the longest I'd ever seen her quiet.

I drank my coffee and chewed at the sandwich. The coffee needed sugar. The roast beef was tough, the lettuce wilted, the bread dried out. I set it on the floor under the chair and went to the bathroom.

The bathroom stank of stale perfume and cigarettes. The floor in front of the toilet was pock marked with cigarette burns. The sink hung from the wall, the spigots gone. A plastic cup dangled from a wire on the back of the toilet. Cora was drinking out of the toilet like a cat.

I heard her move. I looked at my watch. 8:30. She opened her eyes and groaned like an athlete after a hard game.

She sat up. The black lace slip slid higher over her thighs. Sitting on the edge of the bed, she hung her head between her legs and threw up. I watched the yellow dribble onto the floor. She looked up at me. There was pain in her eyes like she'd been drinking broken glass.

Hi Sis, I said.

Toby, she said. What the hell are you doing here? The emptiness in her eyes scared me.

I'll help you get to the bathroom, I said.

I'll do it myself.

But she sat there until I took her arm. She was trembling. We made it around the puke and I sat her down on the toilet then went to the closet again. I dumped the rags out of the cardboard box and tore the box up and spread it over the vomit. I retrieved the coat from the floor and draped it over her shoulders.

She was still sitting on the toilet, bent over, her hands folded across her knees, forehead resting on her hands.

I need a boost, she said.

I held out the coffee. She looked at it like it was something you don't step on.

Sorry Sis, I'm not the man.

If you came here to save my soul, forget it.

Who whipped you? I pointed at the welts.

A guy. He pays for it.

Her voice was thin and raspy. I made a second offering of the coffee. She pitched it on the floor.

I guess you won't feel like eating either, I said.

Go home and let me get on with my life.

She let out a long whish of breath and got up and wobbled to the bed and knelt and poked around for a bit before dragging out a red metal suitcase on a chain hooked to the bed frame.

In the suitcase, there were clothes, a couple pairs of high heeled shoes, stockings, underwear. A box of 100 Lifestyle condoms. A syringe.

While I watched she fed her monkey through a vein in a spider web tattooed on her left breast. She spiked the vein leaving a little red dot like a spider's eye that joined the other needle marks in the web. It made me sick to watch.

Now you're doing junk.

Did I ask you to come here, Toby?

She rubbed her breast where the needle had bitten her and then she stood up and shed the black slip, kicked it into the suitcase with her left foot and then she lifted a towel from the suitcase and went into the bathroom. With her back to me she dipped the cloth in the tank of the toilet and washed her face and under her arms and she wiped between her legs.

My sister. A woman used to being naked in front of men. I wasn't used to seeing her naked. But I didn't matter. I was a pair of eyes attached to a head that belonged to a boy she used to know by the name of Toby. The little brother. I didn't stop watching. She stepped into lace underpants with a little red bow at the waist. She put on a black brassiere with red flowers over the nipples. I watched her tug on black stockings. I watched her slither into a black leather skirt.

Then, sitting on the bed, she opened a black sack purse, took out a compact with a mirror, and uncapped a tube of ultra red lipstick that she spread over her bruised lips. Then she lined on purple mascara until the face was pink and white and red and purple and she smiled in the mirror and clicked the compact shut. You didn't learn that in the Valley, I said.

Go home, Toby. I'm going to work.

You don't ever have to work again, Sis, I said.

The way I said it my voice came out phony. She looked at me, lips pouting ultra crimson and wet. Her eyes were deep purple so the mouse blended into the mascara.

What?

Chuck died and he named you and me and Mickey in his will.

When?

A month ago. Cardiac arrest, heart attack, you know.

Better late than never.

You didn't leave a forwarding address.

She sat on the bed and crossed her legs. They were good legs, my sister's legs.

How much is that asshole worth to me?

125 K, I said. But there's a kicker.

With Chuck there had to be.

To get it, you stay clean for a year.

Shit.

She took a pack of Philippine Tabacaleras out of the sack purse. Black tobacco that burned with the heavy odor of a forest fire.

What kind of shit did he make you eat?

To get mine I had to find you.

Chuck. She looked at me.

He didn't love me, Cora.

She sat there smoking. Quiet. She crossed and recrossed her legs. The street song of flesh in nylon. I heard high heels working their way down the hallway and then the door opened. A tall black woman in purple leather pants and a gold lamé bustier stood in the doorway.

Well, hello darlin, she said, I didn't know you was already on the job.

Allie, this's Toby. Leave us alone, okay?

I'd love to honey, Allie said, but I got a delivery for you.

She stepped over the spilled coffee without even looking at it. Life running on normal for Allie. She handed Cora a package the size of a deck of playing cards. It was wrapped in aluminum foil.

Jason say for you to hold this til he acks you for it.

She smiled at me on her way out.

Cora slipped the foil package into her purse.

Toby, she said, sit beside me.

Her voice was that raspy whiskey baritone some women get when they smoke too much. I sat beside her, smelled her smoke. smelled her perfume. I liked her perfume. I liked everything but the bruises.

We've gotta talk, little brother, she whispered.

She put her hand on my arm and squeezed and then she kissed me on the lips. Her taste came raw and hard through the sharp tang of tobacco. I pulled away. She smiled, her eyes hooded, mouth open. She was searching me and I knew what she was looking for. The cigarette still smoldered in her hand. Things I hadn't felt for a long time boiled up and I knew the real reason I had hunted her down and it didn't have much to do with Chuck.

I was shaking hard but I couldn't admit it so I said the first thing that came into my head.

The last time you touched me was my sixteenth birthday. You held me down by the pool, you sat on my chest and gave me my first French kiss.

Turning her head, she blew a smoke ring and then licked her lips. The Tabacalera was a black snake stuck in a ruby nest.

I remember. You had a hard on that made you blush. You were skinny then, you're not skinny now.

Yeah, not skinny now.

I got up off the bed and retreated to the safety of the chair. I grabbed hold of it and locked my ankles around the legs and kept talking.

All of this. You know. Just happening like this. Mom dying. Chuck. You know, you put up with so much crap, then this comes along. Money falls out of the sky.

She stood up and, moving like a hot oily cloud, closed the gap between us.

I've got a proposition, Toby, she whispered.

She leaned down, her arms snaking around my neck, until her mouth was right against my ear.

What?

Let me have 50 grand, right now, and you can take the rest of my share.

It doesn't work that way.

It's my money. I can do what I want to with it.

I smelled her body. I smelled the nylon and the leather and odors rising up from between her breasts. I could almost smell her thoughts.

You can't touch it for a year.

Where there's money, there's a way.

Cora's voice was a soft cobra rising out of a snake charmer's basket. She straightened up and crushed the cigarette on the floor. She bent down, she put her right index finger under my chin and pulled my head up.

Now, what will it take?

Her breasts in the red fluffy blouse were two inches from my mouth. I took a deep breath and savored the odors. I had to fight myself to keep from taking up her offer.

It's not built that way. My voice was tight, like I had a cold. It's all or nothing. You know Chuck.

That prick! Cora exploded to her feet. Her scents, the perfume, the sweat eddied over me. I sat back and sucked it in. I let her flow into my lungs. I let her anger and her smells kick me in the belly and then I swallowed and looked at her lines—purple, red, the lips, the hips.

I hated his guts from the day mom dragged him into the house. I should have killed him when I was sixteen.

She turned her back to me. The black leather skirt was shiny. The red hair glinted in the dull light, it hung down to her shoulders in curls.

It hadn't been easy being little brother to a big sis like Cora. When she was sixteen she got pregnant. She wouldn't say who by. Chuck tried to beat it out of her. Chuck was a big, strong man and I was afraid of him. Mom and I stood there and watched. I kept telling myself I had to do something, but I didn't. He knocked her down. She got up. He knocked her down again, screaming, and then he quit screaming and just hit her.

She was strong but Chuck was stronger and because he was strong he always got what he wanted. But she never said who the father was. Maybe she didn't know. Chuck ran her over to Calexico for an abortion. I don't know what happened while they were gone but a couple weeks after they got back, Chuck bought her a BMW. Pink. She loved pink.

The day she turned seventeen Cora ran away. She took off in her pink BMW with the black mechanic from

Hermann's Autowerk. She was gone a week. Chuck paid men to hunt her down. Then Chuck paid the men to break the mechanic's legs. He never came back to Indio.

Cora was pacing. Nervous. I watched. I waited.

There's got to be a way, she said.

Mullally's the attorney, Sis, I said, he's rock hard and honest. To get the money...

I don't need Chuck's stinking money. I can make my own money.

How long you gonna last doing this?

You've never been on the street.

You'll get HIV and then what?

Outside, on the street, the action picked up. Cars, heels clicking on the sidewalk, sirens. Car doors slamming. Music. Voices. The symphony of the night.

I reached into my coat pocket and pulled out an envelope. Handed it to her.

What's this?

Terms.

What does that mean?

It's all there. Read it.

She ripped the envelope, flicked the paper out and spread it up against the wall. She went over it, her finger moving on the words, pinning them down.

When she looked up at me, her mouth was tight and hard.

Toby, you're a smug little shit, you know that? You've always been a smug little shit.

Chuck wrote the will.

The son of a bitch.

We've got until Friday. I leave on Friday. I've got a room at the Hilton. 317. Call me.

I left her holding Mullally's paper, I left her standing there, one leg cocked out, the black leather skirt drawn tight across her thighs, her breasts, snugged up from below, flowing out the top of the red blouse with frills on it.

***

On the street, Allie waited. In the yellow light of the street lamp her skin was gray with splotches of white where her make-up glistened.

Hi lover, she said, for twenty bucks I'll suck your dick.

Sorry, Allie, not in the mood.

She smiled. Her lips parted on white teeth with yellow stains. I saw that Allie was a man.

***

At the hotel, I put in a call to Mullally that I'd found Cora and another to the desk to ask for a wake up jingle in the morning. I had just hit the deck when the phone rang. It kept ringing. I answered it.

Cora's voice was huffy like she'd been running.

They won't let me come up.

How are you dressed, Cora?

Toby...

Let me talk to the clerk.

In two minutes, Cora was in the room. Loaded. I knew by the smoothness of her walk and the eyes. Junkies' eyes are a clock on the last pop.

You decided?

Tell me one more time. She snapped the envelope against her legs. All this legal crap. I can get a lawyer.

You can't. If you contest it, the money stays in trust forever. Every time you cop a john's knob, you'll know it's there. Every time you skin pop with a dirty needle, you'll think of that 125 thousand dollars. But you won't ever get it unless you sign. One year from the day you sign Mullally's paper, you bank 125K.

Cora lit a Tabacalera. She smoked and looked at her fingernails. Her face was tight, but the fight was gone out of her.

God damn it Toby, I can't just quit.

Do you want to, I said.

***

I got her a room next to mine. I stayed awake for a couple hours wondering if she'd be there in the morning. She was. Over toast and coffee she told me about Jason and the little package she was carrying.

He's a mean son of a bitch. He'll follow us all the way to Indio and he'll kill me when he catches up.

Why didn't you leave that crap with Allie?

It's junk, Toby.

Give it to me.

Why?

Give me the package.

I held out my hand. She reached into that black sack and then she let out a sigh and looked at me again and then she laid the packet in my hand.

Chuck beat her. I was there, little brother pimping her to Chuck so I could rake in my Judas coin. It would cost him one hundred twenty-five thousand dollars. Three hundred forty-two dollars a day. Fourteen dollars an hour. She looked at the packet in my hand. Her shoulders caved in.

He's still fucking us both, she said.

***

We left Kansas City at ten o'clock after the stores opened. I bought her jeans and a chambray shirt. Sunglasses. We looked like a couple of tourists. All she needed was a camera.

For fourteen hours on the Kansas Turnpike she huddled against the door of the car. She moved only when we stopped for gas. In Amarillo, my neck stiffened so we checked into a room in the Lone Star Motel. The motel had wagon wheels for fence posts and hand painted pictures of the Grand Canyon on the walls.

***

Cora wanted to be strong, but she broke down as soon as we walked into that room. The door closed and she was all over me begging for Jason's junk.

Just a skin pop, she said.

The sweat ran off her. She was clawing at me, clawing at the wall, clawing at the air. The pain had grown fangs.

I knew I'd give in.

She needed it. She was too shaky to do it herself. She bounced over to the bed. Her face white, hands trembling. Hurry, she whispered. I juiced the rig. She stripped off her jeans and rolled over. I found a vein in the back of her knee. She sighed when I slid the needle into her. The needle was her real lover, the one with the eternal hard-on, coming in her. She let her breath out in slow stutters.

My fingers slid to her cheek and then to her neck. She groaned. She stiffened her legs, then her arms, then the rush hit her. She stretched out on her belly on the bed. She rolled over, spreading her red hair out on the pillow. She raised her knees. Her belly was flat and white. Her thighs smooth. She stretched. She got that liquid cat look in her eyes.

Toby, she said, remember the swimming pool, baby? Remember?

She clutched my hand. She licked my fingers like a cat grooming itself and then she sucked my fingers into her mouth, two fingers, working her tongue and teeth against my skin.

With her left hand, she inched the zipper loose on my pants. I should have pulled away, but I just stood there letting her do it. She reached inside my shorts. I was already hard. She dragged me down on the bed.

She inched her black panties to one side. I wanted to look away, but I just stared at her. She guided my hand between her legs. She was wet.

I'll make you come, Toby, make you come, baby.

I kissed her. While I was kissing her, I thought about Mullally then I thought about her legs and I thought about the black panties. He didn't have to know anything. No one had to know anything. I thought about Chuck's money. I lay down beside her and looked at that face and that hair.

Tell me what you like, Toby, she whispered.

My mouth covered hers. I was in her.

When I woke up it was eleven o'clock. I was sweating. I heard a car door slam. Cora lay beside me. She looked rough. Her mouth was open and she drooled on her pillow. Her hair was matted with sweat. We smelled of sex. It wasn't a bad smell. I knew I could get used to it.

Footsteps outside the door. Fist pounding. My heart kicked up a notch.

I got up. I grabbed Jason's packet.

Cora sat up.

Where are you going?

To let him in, I said.

No, she said. Don't. Please.

I can buy him off, I said.

He'll kill me.

Like you said, Cora, if you got money there's a way.

And then I unhooked the chain.

Bad Debt

It felt like ice—cold at first.

Then, warming against my teeth.

Metal. Long, hard steel strong enough to take the pressure.

The barrel settled against my teeth clicking like a rattle snake.

I took a deep breath. The curve of the trigger is smooth round slick and wet as a just-kissed mouth.

I never liked the taste of metal when I was a kid. The sharp electric jolt through your molars when you bit into aluminum foil spoiled me for it.

The taste of steel, though, at this point in my life, was sweet because I don't like pain and they had said there would be pain.

No one really intends to do it, Alvarez said. Well. The taste of steel in your mouth is about as real as anything gets when you're on the edge.

I've been there for six months now. On the edge.

I closed my eyes. Visualize. What happens? My head blown off. Freedom.

This is the fourth time I've sat on the edge.

Once in Mother's pickup out on the ranch. Midnight.

Once beside the black walnut trees on the Kings River.

Once in the bedroom at Nancy's on New Year's Eve.

And this one, waiting alone in Nancy's Pontiac at eight-thirty p.m. on a moonless night in February for the angels of death to come and take their god-damned money.

Violence.

It's in my blood. I've been violent since I was little. Take what I wanted, when I wanted, to hell with everyone else. Some things you don't take, though, like another man's money. Sleep with his wife, steal his car, shoot his dog—but his money?

You do that you pay back blood. And they wanted blood. My blood.

It's the violence of fire or the rapid red violence of blood spilling out like water from a broken main. It's always about violence.

I felt like an animal on a log floating on a flooding river then.

Something catches in your throat when you see it so clear—you know nothing can save you from excesses you didn't see as extreme. Then you grow up. You learn. They do you or you do yourself and so you leap into the water. What the hell.

I've always hated being helpless.

The first time they broke my pinky. Next time, they said, it's your leg and then your head and after that we cut you up and feed you to the dogs.

The broken bone set. It was on my right hand, my good hand.

The second time, on the Kings River, I wasn't in enough pain. Just thinking about one of them breaking my head almost sent me over the edge, but I didn't do it then.

The third time, they didn't crack my skull, they cracked my leg in two places. Next time though it'll be your head, they told me. One of them wanted to slice pieces of my face off right then, but no, save it for next time.

When you're helpless, you'll try anything—or you give up. I was there. Try anything or give up.

I sat on the bed in Nancy's bedroom on New Years Eve tasting steel, trying to find the guts to pull the trigger when she walked in.

She wasn't shocked or amazed or even curious. She knew. Getting in trouble. That's what I specialized in. What'd you get yourself into this time, little brother? she said. She always took care of me. Even when we were little she was there with a dime to buy candy and later, in high school it was five bucks to pay off a bad roll of the dice, but this time she was as helpless as I was. How can you stop the sun from rising?

I told her. She listened. Sat with me like a confessor then took the .38 and nestled it in her lap and snuggled against me. I won't let anything happen to you, she said. How much do you owe them?

I can't do this, I said. It'll ruin you.

How much?

It's nasty, I told her.

It's just money, she said.

So she bailed me out again, not all the way but far enough for the log I was riding on to rise up and out of the water a little bit. Now I owe her and I owe them and they'll want blood.

Some people have a genius for getting into trouble. That's me. I don't intend to. It builds up and pretty soon

I'm careening down an arroyo one step ahead of a flash flood and there's no way in hell I can out run it.

I invented the law of unintended consequences, sort of like the guys who built the first atom bomb without thinking it through. It catches up with you, not thinking. A broken finger here, a cracked leg, a couple of cities blown all to hell, your finger on the trigger of a blue steel .38. Why?

The windows of Nancy's Pontiac steam up. I'm anxious, breathing too much for a dead man. Breathe a little less,· live a little longer. It's cold and wet and I'm afraid. I settle down with the .38, feel its comforting curves, a true, a good friend.

Nine p.m.. Ten p.m. The Pontiac smells like a tomb.

Lights pop up in the mirror at ten-thirty. Head-lights. I cock the .38.

Snugged up behind me, the black car—can't tell if it's a Lincoln or a Chrysler—waits like a vulture, headlights on, exhaust boiling up behind and around and over it. I see faces in the mirror, masks like skeletons in a Day of the Dead parade. Then the headlights die.

Ahead of me, at the corner, another black car blocks the alley.

Crosswise. Son of a bitch.

Headlights off, it waits for me.

I've counted the bills. Hundreds. I'm short. Fifty one hundred dollar bills short. I've sold my wreck of a car, hocked everything left, taken Nancy's money that mother left her and I'm still five thousand bucks short.

Money.

A door opens behind me. I'm squeezed between twin black anvils.

A man walks to the passenger door of the Pontiac, raps on the window.

Hey, he says. Hey.

Like a secret, I aim the .38 at the door.

Give it, he says. He grins. Bad teeth. Bad man. Bad suit.

No, I say.

What?

I lower the window half-way with the power button. The whir of motors a comfort like a robot coming alive.

No, I say.

Look, he says.

Bite it, I say.

It's your head, pardner, he says.

Wait, I say.

What?

I'm short, I say.

You come up short last time, he says.

What?

He leans over, speaks through the gap in the window. I smell his cologne. Bad cologne. The kind you buy in a drugstore. His eyes shine.

I said you come up short last time. There ain't no other time so let's go.

Hey, I say. He tries the door handle.

What?

He leans down again. I lift the .38 and shoot him in the face and he rocks back. The explosion fills the Pontiac. I drop it into gear. Lurch forward. Then spin the wheel like I know what I'm doing and come around slewing to face the black car behind me. A Lincoln. As I spin, the door opens and two men pile out and I shoot at them. I roll past. They fire at me but what the hell and then there is a sharp hard bite that drives me into the steering wheel....

Where am I going?

I'm in over my head now, so far over my head and the log I jumped off of is bearing down on me at a hundred miles an hour and there is a cataract in this river and it's four miles high and there's no shut off valve on this baby.

The whip of cold air through the open glass, the whine of cold air through the Pontiac is freezing. I'm lost now. I've always been lost, from the beginning, but I'm lost and sunk now. It's just a matter of time.

At the corner of Railroad Avenue and Commerce, there is a bar.

It is not a good bar.

It is the last bar on the last corner on the last street on the road to hell.

But the whiskey tastes fine.

My left arm is numb.

My breath stinks.

But the whiskey....

Johnny Walker? The bartender says, In here you get Old Crow.

Fine, I say. Whiskey. Good.

Are you all right?

No, I think I'm shot dead.

Oh, he says.

He backs away from my blood, Old Crow fifth still in hand. Don't bring your shit in here.

Too late. Too damn late. It's here.

Get the hell outta here.

But the door opens and two men enter. They are ugly. They come from ugly stock. Their fathers were ugly and their mothers were ugly and they married ugly women who bore them children as ugly as half-assed bulldogs and the pistols in their hands are ugly and the bartender says, Get your ass outta here, all of you bozos.

Shut your mouth, one of the men says.

The bartender is a man who could be my brother. He takes care of me. There are heavy explosions like cannons in my head, all around me and there are dull grunts, the sounds men make when they are mortally wounded, and the sound of meat hitting wood and the bartender says, God damn it.

I look through smoke and taste gunpowder and see the blue glint of the barrel of a shotgun—ugly—and the two men are piles of gabardine and wool on the floor beside the jukebox where Floyd Cramer plays a long, very long medley of songs about death and dying.

Now you get your scrawny little ass out of here, the bartender says.

There are more of them, I say. There's a whole army of them.

He points the shotgun at me. He says,

Yeah, and they'll want a piece of me after they finish chewing your legs off. Did you hear me?

Yes, sir, I say.

I limp out, still smelling the gun-powder.

Outside the bar, the Pontiac stood doors open. Behind it, the black Lincoln. In the Lincoln a single face.

I walk to the Lincoln. The man inside rolls down his window. He grins.

We've got your sister, he says.

So I shoot him in the neck and go to the Pontiac and sit there in the cold until there are sirens.

Mildred

She arched a crooked eyebrow and looked at me over her glasses. Pink, swoopy glasses, the kind that went out of style just before the Cuban missile crisis. She was named Mildred and she talked like an unreconstructed sailor who'd never heard of Gloria Steinem.

Her language was full of body parts and different physical ducts, and the things you were supposed to do with them. It was enough to make your tongue freeze up and turn your face pink and make you think that maybe Irishmen or Arabs or Spaniards, born to foul language, were Sunday school teachers.

But not in Kansas No one swore in Kansas. Mildred made up for every minister's wife's purity by getting even with the dictionary.

We had met in the bar on a train coming back from Wichita and I watched her belt three straight shots of bourbon before I made my move.

I figured that a woman who could snort Wild Turkey with that kind of finesse didn't deserve to travel by herself. So I told her the usual lies, gave her my mechanic's address and phone number.

She lifted that eyebrow again. I gulped down the Wild Turkey and lit a cigarette.

Mildred, crossed her legs and cocked one knee up on the bar.

You like chicken soup? she asked me.

175

Chicken soup?

From chicken entrails. Gizzards and liver and lungs. On the farm, she said, we used the entrails after we'd shipped all the other parts to the packer. Times were tough. We lived on chicken soup.

You lived on chicken soup? I said. Doesn't seem to have slowed you down.

Yeah, she belted her fourth Wild Turkey and teetered a little.

I like you Mildred, I said. I like you, but I'm getting off this train in Liberal.

She leaned back, put her hands on the bar and rocked the stool to the beat of the wheels knocking on the rails.

I'm going on to Meade, she said, but let me give you my address and you come and see me sometime.

She handed me a slip of paper. Mildred Collins, it said. I remembered a Margaret Collins. I went to high school with her. We got together at the fair and rode the big ferris wheel. We went steady for a year. I took the address and put it in my wallet.

***

Three weeks later I made a stop through Meade and looked Mildred up.

She was the head of a big nursing home on the outskirts of town. The home was full of grandmothers who couldn't remember their names or the names of their children and they called the nurses Momma.

When I walked in on Mildred she was sitting at her desk wearing a pair of red silk pants. She had on black shoes and black stockings and a bright gold blouse.

The pink swoopy glasses were cocked up on top of her head and her mouth glowed a bright red streak that parted two rows of the whitest teeth I'd seen in a long time.

Who the hell are you? she snapped as I shut the door behind me and plopped into a chair.

Willy Jones.

You lyin' sack of shit, she said, I called that number you gave me and got Fred's Auto Shop. You asshole...

Now look, Mildred. I apologize. I was...

You are a slimy little piece of shit.

But I came to see you didn't I?

***

So I took her out to dinner at a place called Patagonia. We had steak and lobster and baked potatoes with melted cheese on them. The waiter brought a little container of condiments and Mildred heaped huge glops of sour cream and green onions on her potatoes. Then she reared back, knocked down the third Wild Turkey and took on the steak.

Damn, could that lady eat. I put the lobster down on top of half a carafe of a pretty good cabernet for Kansas and helped myself to a little kneesy with Mildred. She grinned over the steak and grabbed my hand across the table and said: Will, I like you even if you are a lying son of a bitch.

I came back, Mildred, I said, I couldn't get you out of my mind.

You are a lying sack of shit and you know it. You remembered me in that bar on the train and you thought Old Millie will roll over like a pole-axed ox and I'll bet she gives good head besides.

No way, I said. I thought about you in the bar of that train, and I said to myself that I had to see you again because of the chicken entrails...

Chicken entrails?

Did you really eat chicken entrail soup?

You're a born snake oil salesman Willy, she said when she could breathe again. I can spot them like bad grapes or a fox in a hen house.

Aw Mildred, I scoffed and tried to look humble and embarrassed and cute all at the same time, but she had my number.

The only thing I remembered about Mildred was her Wild Turkey and the pink glasses and the bare legs against the bar.

Until I walked into the nursing home that morning, I'd forgotten how tall she was, what color her hair was and everything else about her. I had remembered that she was female. She lit a cigarette and looked at me, her eyes narrowed.

Well, she said, you got a lock on it?

On what?

The door of the motel room?

Mildred, I didn't come here for that.

Like hell you didn't. She lifted a glass and the light caught her eyes, they glistened and I saw some deep playfulness there.

Okay, I said, I've had the hots for you ever since that day on the train. I came here to see if we could take a little day trip over to the lake and lie in the sun and look at our navels.

Good god, she said, I offer you a piece of the finest ass in Kansas and you go gazonga about your navel. What in the hell is the matter with you Willy?

I think I just remembered the combination to the lock, I said.

178

She smiled, she reached into her purse, she tossed a set of keys at me. She said,

You drive, I give directions.

Mildred reminded me of my first wife and maybe that's why I went to Meade in the first place.

She was quiet when she made love but very intense. She was the finest piece of ass in Kansas. As far as I knew.

When are you coming through here again, Willy? She asked later.

I'm tired right now, Mildred, I said, and I forgot the combination again. I was getting dense now that the fire had been put out. She laughed. She said,

Roll over here and kiss me, you little shit.

I'm going to Plains next week, I said. Then I'll drop in if you want me to.

Of course I want you to. She pulled me down beside her and then whispered, Willy, I need a shot of that Turkey.

I jumped up and poured the juice into a glass with some ice. She sipped it then hit it hard and held it out to me. Hit me again Willy, she said.

You can work out of here as easy as you can out of Liberal, Mildred said. Who's going to know anyway?

I had been coming through Meade for six months and in that time I had started staying with Mildred and then one day, even though I couldn't say it, I knew I didn't want to leave her.

She had a big laughing way of getting inside of me and after two months she had quit calling me a sneaky little shit. I kind of missed it.

I noticed the change in her too about the same time. I'd come into town and she'd have had her hair done, new clothes, lipstick in shade of chinese red and deep purple. She was painting herself and I loved it.

She started wearing dresses all the time we were together and she took off her high heels so she wasn't taller than I was. We went dancing, so I guess you could say it was serious.

You mean move in here? With you? I said.

I mean if you don't want to, she said.

***

Things changed. Mildred was a handful but I got to enjoy her craziness the way you enjoy rich food and good bourbon. I came in one day from a bad trip to Hutchison and Mildred was sitting in a chair at the kitchen table and I noticed that the swoopy glasses were gone.

Mildred, I said, where are the pink swoopies?

She grinned at me. Willy, I'm a new woman. I got contacts. See what you did for me?

Her eyes were violet. Before they had been green.

I'll be damned, I said.

I came home one day from a hellish trip to Quapaw Oklahoma and Millie was standing at the kitchen sink and when she turned around, I saw that she had cut her hair.

You like it?

I like it, I said, but I was getting a little bit worried because there wasn't much left of the woman from the train.

One Friday, I blew into town in a new T Bird I bought with a big bonus from selling a dozen header seeders to one of the corporate ranches and Milly was sitting in an easy chair watching TV. I leaned over to kiss her and saw that she had braces on her teeth.

It was hard kissing her then because her wires kept poking my tongue and my lips. It did the same thing to her, so pretty soon, we weren't kissing anymore.

I lay in bed waiting for her and she came out of the bathroom and sat down on the bed and started to trim her toenails.

I've been thinking, Willy, she said, I think I want to get liposuction on this gut of mine.

I like your gut, Mildred, I said.

You'd like me better if I didn't pooch out in front.

Mildred, sweetheart, there ain't nothing left of you.

I know it Willy, she said, but I can't stop now.

She didn't.

She didn't stop with liposuction. She had her nose done, her lips puffed, her hairline realigned. She had liposuction on her thighs and on her butt. Every time I came home, there was a stranger in my bed.

Willy, she said, one Saturday as we were lying in bed eating waffles and sucking strawberries and peaches, I've been thinking that maybe I ought to learn French.

Honey, if you want to learn French, then by god, you ought to do it.

So she did. Eight months later she spoke French like a Parisienne.

I was getting uneasy after all of this because my trips were getting longer. They wanted me to move to the head office in Topeka.

I came home one day and Millie was sitting in a chair at the kitchen table.

Willy, she said, I've found someone else.

I figured you would, sweetheart, I said. Do you want me to leave?

You can stay as long as you like, Willy. We just can't sleep together anymore. I told him I wouldn't sleep with you.

Nothing new there, I said, I lost the combination to your lock a year ago.

I know, she said, but once I got started, I couldn't stop.

Who is the guy?

My surgeon, she said, his mother is in the home and we sort of got to know one another.

Kids? All doctors got kids.

Four, but I'll get used to it.

I moved out the next week-end, took the promotion to Topeka and now I have the whole Western half of the US. Good company, John Deere.

Phone Call

I call her every morning. Today, yesterday, the day before.

I'm hemorrhaging, she says when I ask how she is. I changed my dosage of progestin and now...

How bad is it? I ask her.

The doctor said a super tampax an hour is a pretty bad sign.

Well, I say. You know you're not pregnant. She laughs

I have called her every day for a year except Christmas. I call because she said I need to hear your voice, I really need to see you, to feel you, but the voice will keep me going.

She's like that. She's in pain now. Sometimes when we talk, I almost see her eyes narrow—I can feel the pulse of pain in her body, her voice tries to mask it, but the hesitation before she swallows tells me the eyes are narrow with pain and the hand moves to the flat belly, pressing. I call her every day for the report.

One day I'll call and Michael will answer or Ali will say, Who is this? And I will hang up—I dread that day, the empty hollowness of a throb in my throat. But for now, the phone rings, she answers, and for a moment, as I say her name, I hear a sigh—and she says, I was afraid you wouldn't call. Michael and I are fighting again over silly things. Last night at the neighborhood party, he

183

went on and on about the wine—imagine the wine. There are so many things to be upset about and he focuses on the wine. Why do you suppose he does that?

How are you? I ask. I need to hear about you, not about him. Nothing about him.

I'm hurting, today, she says. I couldn't sleep last night.

The pulse in my neck quickens. I remember our first meeting, at a safe distance—across the airport waiting room—I felt her the way you feel the rush of air when a car sweeps past you on the street. The first minute was mute—a silent movie from the golden age—a sign of recognition in the eyes full of Spring, and the hands exploring fingers—before the first eruption of, God, so this is you?

I imagine our second meeting on the beach in Santa Monica in full sun, her skin golden, the small hairs on her thighs taking the light like prisms. She wore a black dress that bared her shoulders and rode up on her thighs to take the sun.

There is a space between us. A gnawing space between us, a deep gnawing space between us. I hear it in her voice—but the thousand miles between Los Angeles and Seattle vanish when the phone clicks and she says—Hello. The distance between us is thick with bodies and a husband, and children and family—an aging mother, a sick father about to have a shunt implanted to solve his failing kidney problem—family, and a Wheaton terrier named Rex. Road blocks more bitter than tank traps.

I always have this fantasy when we're on the phone—I walk through the gate at the back of the house on Latimer Road and I close it quietly the way you close a door when a child is sleeping...

Are <u>you</u> all right? she asks.

Yes, I say, tell me what the doctor said.

As she talks, I see Michael beside the pool, Rex on a white lawn chair sleeping, and as I approach, I see that Michael lies on the concrete rim of the pool, his head split open.

A stream of blood pours — surreal—into the pool darkening it. As the blood swirls, the pool turns the color of cherry jello.

What are you working on? she asks me. Are you working on something?

I'm always working on something, I tell her. I squat beside Michael, feel his pulse. He is still warm, Rex looks at me. He whines—he recognizes me from the week-end visits—and I close my eyes. If Michael were dead, life would be simpler.

You sound distant today, she says.

I'm wandering, I tell her.

What?

Nothing.

Tell me.

Just the vision again.

Well. She laughs. You're the last person to want him dead, aren't you?

Yes, I say, you don't kill a man if you're sleeping with his wife.

If you slept with his wife, past tense, she says. But then, there's no proof, is there?

Pause.

It's been so long. Why does it have to be so long? I can't stand the thought of never seeing you again.

I wait. There is nothing to do but wait when she starts this particular rant. If she rants about Michael, or

185

her father's illness, or Ali, I will interrupt, redirect her the way you redirect a small child who wants a piece of candy or a doll at a toy store—but when she begins this particular tirade, I wait. Nothing will stop her until the final, accusatory—You don't love me. You never loved me. You never want to see me again.

I wait, take the deep, quieting breath, then—You know the facts as well as I do. We can't rewrite history.

Fifty percent of all marriages in LA end in divorce, she says.

You know my guilt complex is too strong for that.

You're just looking at your check book, she says. I have money. I'll have money when Sam dies, when Cecile dies.

I wait. She lists the accounts, the amounts. We have worked on this so many times I know the script. I know how much she is worth. I wait. She pauses for a breath. I say, Yes, but I can't, I can't, I can't...

She jiggles the phone. Makes it rattle the way she does when we reach this impasse.

You just can't stand the idea of being with a dying woman, can you? she says.

I wait. I see Michael on the concrete, Rex in the chair—blood in the water, policemen coming through the gate to arrest me.

I say, You know that is not why.

She hisses at me. She says, You are a miserable liar. If it weren't for the voice, I'd never talk to you again.

It will never end happily. I know it won't. It can't. How can it?

She cries. Her voice shrinks until there are just sobs. My heart quickens. I want to hold her. To tell her things.

I wait. Then, her deep cleansing breath. She has control of herself again. My heart slows down.

Aren't you tired of me whining all the time? she asks.

She is like that—so brave. Shattered, she lives in a body that breaks small piece by small piece—blood filled with sugar, brittle diabetes she calls it. The bleeding, the pain—she is like that. One night, in complete surrender, after we made love, she told me there was something wrong with her.

What is wrong with you? I asked her.

I'm fatally optimistic, she said. It's impossible for me to look at the dark side. I leave that to you, the poets.

She is empty now, talked out, tired, tears dried, she waits.

I say, I'll call you tomorrow.

I know, she whispers.

Are you all right?

Do you care? She spits at me.

You know I do.

She laughs.

You called. I'm fine. I'll survive. I'm a survivor. I've survived everything. Even losing you.

I hang up.

Tomorrow I will phone again. I expect it to ring and Michael or Ali will answer and ask, Who is this? When that happens, I will hang up knowing that there can be no more calls.

Today, however, she sounds like sunshine on ripe mangos. That is good.

www.ingramcontent.com/pod-product-compliance
Lightning Source LLC
Chambersburg PA
CBHW060814120626

46557CB00001B/206